NEW YORK TIMES & USA TODAY BESTSELLING AUTHOR

NICOLE BLANCHARD

TRAITOR

A LAST TO LEAVE NOVEL

Traitor

Copyright © 2018 by Nicole Blanchard

Bolero Books LLC
11956 Bernardo Plaza Dr. #510
San Diego, CA 92128
www.buybolerobooks.com

CONTENTS

For Michelle

PAST - SOMEWHERE IN THE FUCKIN' DESERT

DESPITE IT BEING hot as the devil's ballsack, my guts twist with an icy apprehension that can't mean anything good.

There's nothing as far as my night vision goggles can see but dust, scrubby little plants, and huge towering dunes. The village we're surveying is dead quiet, which should be reassuring, but it isn't. It makes years of instincts honed by training scream with unease.

A cold sweat coats my back, reminding me all too vividly of the time we were ambushed on my first deployment, which feels like a lifetime ago. I'd had the same frozen ball of dread in my stomach then, too. I had no sway as a grunt then. I couldn't tell my command we should turn

1

back because I was worried. I couldn't have saved my friend Scott, who lost a leg on that mission and nearly lost his life.

But I can today.

In the years since the explosion, I've been deployed multiple times. I rose in the ranks in the infantry until I joined the Marine Special Operations Command (MARSOC) as an operator. The day Scott was injured didn't only change his life. It changed mine, too. I'd been coasting along in the military, uncertain what I wanted, where I was going. When I woke up in a German hospital with a severe concussion and a broken arm with my friend hovering near death, I knew one thing: I wouldn't let it happen to anyone else.

I was a headstrong shit back then, that's for damn sure.

Because if I've learned anything it's that no one but no one can control what happens under the cover of night. Not even the men with guns and enough tactical training to choke a camel. I do my level best, though, and I like to think it makes a difference.

On a night like this, it brings to mind all the reasons why running head first into trouble is never a good idea.

But of course, we do it anyway.

I give a prearranged signal to my second in command, Callum "Cal" Reese, who speaks into his mic, directing the rest of the team to their designated checkpoints. Snipers to the high-ground, breachers to the front. The same well-oiled machine we'd become for the past seven months since being assigned to what Cal affectionately dubbed Camp "Hellhole". Each team is different, depending on mission objectives, but five of the guys I've deployed with before. Reuniting with them almost felt like coming home. I'm not sure when an Afghani wasteland started to become my reprieve and home became the place I wanted to escape.

"Creepy," Cal says and I nod in agreement.

"I'd be enthused if it didn't feel like a fucking horror flick."

"Dun-na, dun-na, duna duna duna," comes one of our snipers, Killian "Kill" Burke. His partner James Murdoch sniggers.

Movement from the village quiets us all and in seconds intense focus descends. Our mission for tonight's excursion is to clear the village and capture it for our own, along with any enemy objectives or intel. A second team, led by my good buddy Brian Tate, will be doing the same, but from the South side of the village. I glance back to our intelligence officer and possibly the most intimidating of our team, Dean Tyler, who nods, confirming Tate's signal. Behind him a group of support Marines and Afghani military stand ready. They'll clear each building while we scope ahead for any high value targets.

The squat little buildings are pressed together, some crumbling from decades of neglect and small-level warfare between battling regimes, others have already disintegrated to dust, husks of their former selves. There are times when I get the feeling I'm stuck in an ancient era at the ends of the earth, when you've seen nothing but mud-huts and caves for weeks on end. Probably why going home at the end of each deployment is such a shock.

There's nothing like being covered in blood and brain matter one day and being asked why you aren't laughing along at your welcome home barbecue the next.

I push those thoughts and my own niggling doubts to the back of my mind as we slowly, carefully, move closer to the village. My team and Tate's depends on me to be focused and ready for any eventuality. Including the worst.

Cal arranges himself supine next to my position beside an outcropping of rock just on the perimeter of the village. He readies his high-powered sights and scans the area as I call in an update to the rest of the team and the support fifty yards back positioned in a ravine. When I'm done, I look back to him and he shakes his head.

No outward sign of danger, but that doesn't mean it's not lurking in the shadows waiting for us to make our move.

Most villagers have already abandoned this settlement and the ones who are left sure as hell don't want us coming in and taking over, but we have a job to do and lives are always on the line, on both sides. If we don't move in now, intel villagers have or targets they're hiding may cost lives, both American and foreign. Tens, hundreds, thousands. It's a guessing game, in the end, and we do what we can to protect that loss of life, even if it costs us our own.

"Move out," I order and Cal, Kill, James, and Dean shift in sync without question.

Kill and James crouch down, shadows blending with the pitch dark sky on rooftops in the distance. Cal and I move on opposite ends of the village, followed by Dean in the back with our support.

Seconds after I clear the first line of buildings, shots ring out against the night and I hear a short scream followed by the sound of meat and bone colliding with the hard packed dirt underneath my feet.

"Two guards neutralized," Kill says into the mic, and I don't need the reminder to know he earns his nickname with each mission.

As I progress through the village with a small group of Marines, we clear the buildings one by one. After an hour of this, I start to feel like the mission is a wash. There are no high value targets, no valuable intel to be gleaned. All in all, it's a fairly easy mission compared to most. More importantly, aside from the two kills on the onset, no significant loss of life. Tate's team, according to Cal, reports the same.

The constant rapport of flash-bangs could be heard in the distance as Tate leads his own team in a mirror pattern.

Throughout it all they keep me updated through the mic. Soon, we reached the opposite end of town.

Dean appears, face trickling with sweat and flushed red, followed by Kill and James. Marines and Afghani military crouch beyond, faces bleached of color and drawn from lack of sleep. I don't blame them. I'm going on thirty hours without hitting my bunk, but the only thing you can do is keep pressing forward.

When Tate joins with his team, I turn and signal that we should round up and go back to base. The mission may have been a bust, but there will be another tomorrow and the next day and the next. My guys need to rest and I need to report our findings back to command, even if they're shit.

There's a two mile hike before any rest can be had and that's two miles we'll be navigating in the dark completely vulnerable to attack so I can't quite let down my guard yet.

I slap Tate on the back and say, "Let's get this shit show on the road."

We're halfway back to camp when it all goes to hell.

The first gunshot goes off just as the lights for camp begin to shine on the horizon. Everyone hits the ground, dust flies up and fills my mouth and eyes. I rub a hand over my face and choke. I don't have time to worry about the grit under my lids and coating my tongue.

"We're surrounded," I hear through my radio.

I hear Tate curse from somewhere to my right and the

apprehension I've been feeling all night curdles in my stomach.

Fuck, but, *fuck* I knew this had been a bad idea. Knew it just as I knew we're in deep shit.

Tate radios back to base and Kill and Murdoch murmur in the background as they scout for our best option of retreat.

"To the east," Kill announces into the radio. "There's a break in their line."

"Go," I command Cal. Tate and I stay back to give the Marines and the rest our our Team time to find cover.

Shots pop off, little flashes in the obsidian night. Tate and I shoot at the direction of fire to give our men a chance, any chance. Screams fill what had been an eerily quiet night. My body moves by memory, as my mind races with where we'd gone wrong. This mission was supposed to be an easy in-and-out, if there is such a thing. We'd gotten a tip-off that it'd be ours for the taking. No enemies in the area.

So much for that shit.

"You go up," Tate orders. As my senior in command, I defer to his judgement, but it chaps my ass to leave him vulnerable.

Knowing hesitation or arguments will only cost us both precious time, I sprint up the dunes with Tate close on my heels. Kill and Murdoch have taken up places on the dunes and I hear the silent, deadly hiss of our nation's finest shots whizzing past my ears.

I reach the crest of the dune and toss myself over the edge. Tate is seconds behind me when the blast knocks him off his feet and throws him a dozen yards away.

When the dust settles and I peer over the dune and through my NVGs, I see Tate, well, parts of him, littered over the dusty landscape.

What remains of him peers through the darkness. Bloody froth bubbles at the corners of his mouth as he mouths, "Help me."

PRESENT

My FINGERS TWITCH on the steering wheel, but for the first time, it isn't due to the dark grip of anxiety. It's with the urge to paint, to create. I haven't felt the blessing of inspiration in so long, I tap on the brakes. They squeal and a car behind me honks in protest at my sudden deceleration.

Get it together, Peyton.

I accelerate once more, but commit the location to memory and pull off the next exit from the Blue Ridge Parkway and direct my ancient car toward the town that shares the name of the view—Windy Point, North Carolina.

The stunning landscape keeps pressing me toward the town center. The urge to capture the mix of color, of movement and shadow. *This*. This was what I was looking for. As I pull to a stoplight, I search the town on my phone, excitement bubbling happily in my stomach. The quaint little mountain village of Windy Point boasts a population of less than 2,000 year round. But it's not the variety of tourist attractions, the museums or the multitude of shopping boutiques I'm interested in. It's the openness. The freedom that attracts me. I'm in awe of the sweeping thrust of mountain peaks and the deep blue-green of the oak and hickory forests. The jewel-blue of a sparkling lake peeks out between thick brush as I round a corner and I release the breath I'd been holding since I set out on my journey two weeks and three states ago.

When I'd realized the urge to paint had all but dried up inside of me.

When it felt like the last part of me holding out hope had died.

Realizing I could either wither away and accept the inevitable slow march to death or fight for the life I'd lost, I'd packed what little possessions I could fit into my car and set out in search of something—anything—that could make me *feel* again. Feel in a way that I hadn't in longer than I could remember.

I used to be a big believer in passion, in fate, destiny. *Life*.

I'm determined to find my way back to life even if it kills me.

I'd followed the winding roads from across the country without a destination in mind. Searching for—I wasn't sure what exactly, but I figured I'd know it when I saw it.

For anyone else the journey would have taken less than half a day, but I figure for someone who couldn't even leave her own house six months ago, it was progress. Slow, but progress nonetheless.

For the first time in a long time, I didn't have a plan. I didn't have a structured to-do list to guide my every waking moment or a host of professionals telling me the right way— or the wrong way—to face my demons each day. Supposedly, the years of intense therapy would teach me how to handle my grief, my anxiety, but all it had done was remind me at every session of all that had happened.

Maybe counseling had given me tools to deal with those things, but ultimately, it was the shock of my twenty-eighth birthday that propelled me to make a drastic change. Something about facing the tail end of my twenties and eventual dawn of my thirties had forced me to pull myself out of the mire of my past and do something about it. The only other option was letting it drown me. And I owed it to myself— and to them, to make something of the life I had left.

My heart pounds and I almost giggle in relief, because it doesn't make me want to run for the nearest sanctuary and bolt the doors behind me. Instead, I want to scream and dance. I want to explore and paint—God, I want to paint more than I ever have—even more than *before*.

The exhilaration may fade, but for now, Windy Point is my new beginning, a fresh canvas. As I told my therapist on our monthly check-in, I'm prepared for the worst, but expecting the best. Even if I only stay a night or a week or a month, the change of scenery is what I'm looking for more than anything. I'll get the chance to go back and take in more of the view that inspired me so much, go hiking or swim in the lake if the weather holds up.

I don't need a job, but if my stay lengthens longer than a week, I can visit any one of the touristy places I pass on my way through town for something to keep me busy. A restaurant, or a museum, or one of the boutiques may need some extra help now that the last fingers of winter are beginning to loosen their strangling hold on the surroundings. Visitors will no doubt flock to the area, which will mean a healthy supply of employment opportunities should the need arise.

Dusk sweeps over the nearby peaks and bathes the town at its base in an inky pool of blue-green shadow. There won't be any exploring tonight, but I don't mind. If nothing else, the years spent cooped up with my nightmares taught me to wring every drop of pleasure out of each moment, no matter the circumstances.

A fluorescent sign advertising a 50's style diner named

Lola's catches my eye and my stomach lets out a grumble. Realizing I haven't had anything to eat since Tennessee turned into North Carolina, I flip on my signal and merge over to the right lane to pull into the parking lot. It gives me a little flutter in my chest to realize I have an appetite again. To be excited to eat food to enjoy it and not just for fuel.

Once, not too long ago, the scents of charred meat and grease that greet my nose as I open the diner door would have sent me running in the other direction. Instead, my stomach grumbles again as I walk up to the hostess stand.

A young girl in ill-fitting black pants and a rumpled white button-down shirt greets me with an easy smile. "Evening! How many?"

"Just the one," I answer, returning her smile.

"Right this way."

She guides me through a crush of evening patrons, around a knockout brunette, to a small table in the back of the restaurant. Nerves jangle uneasily in my stomach and my mouth goes dry.

"I'm sorry," I say before she can lead into her spiel about the waitress being with me soon. "Would you mind? I'd love to have a seat in the corner if it isn't any trouble."

The hostess gives me the side-eye, but she acquiesces to my request without comment. The breath I was holding releases when she gestures to a table nearer to the kitchen and therefore less desirable—to anyone else.

"Thank you," I say with feeling. The desire to flee abates. "I appreciate it."

"You're welcome! Your server will be with you in a few minutes to take your order."

Once she leaves, I scan the room automatically, noting the exits, the other customers. I catch myself studying them and have to take another deep breath and to relax. Elvis croons from an old-fashioned juke-box on the opposite side of the restaurant and chrome accents flash from every direction. Humming along with "You Ain't Nothin' But a Hound Dog", I study the menu with keen interest.

Around me waitresses in cute little teal outfits bustle to and from tables, carrying trays filled to the brim with the usual diner fare. Burgers, fries, milkshakes and sodas abound. Everything looks delicious, but I limit myself to a small cherry coke, a small order of fries, and a chicken sandwich when the waitress arrives to take my order.

When she returns, I only have eyes for the plate full of greasy, bad-for-me food. She sets the feast in front of me and I have to clench my hands in my lap to keep from lunging at it. "This looks great, thank you."

She places a straw on the table and retrieves the menu. "New in town?"

Ignoring the gnawing hunger in my stomach, I nod. "Brand new, actually."

"I thought so. Didn't think I've seen you around. I'm Renee. Windy Point native."

I shake the proffered hand. "Peyton, nice to meet you. I'm from all over, I guess."

"Oh? Here on vacation."

I lift a shoulder. "Sort of. My Uncle lives over near Camp Lejeune. I was headed that way when I came across your town. I can't get over the scenery here. It's like living in a fairy tale."

Renee leans a hip on the table, content to chat. Hoping she won't take offense, I nibble on a French fry. "You'll have to go see Windy Point, then. Words don't do it justice. I've lived here all my life and it still takes my breath away."

Thinking of the mountaintops I'd passed, the way the light had played over the trees, I say, "I'll have to do that."

Someone shouts her name and Renee's friendly smile turns into a grimace. "I better get back to work. You'll let me know if you need anything?"

I ginned. "Actually, before you go..."

LATER, I HANG A LEFT ON OLD OAK LANE ON THE northern side of town near the dark glimmer of the lake I'd passed before, christened Bear Lake according to Renee. Huddled around its shores are several bed and breakfasts, cabin rentals, and hotels. After stuffing myself with greasy food, the exhaustion from a long day of driving pulls at my eyelids. I count myself lucky that I do a decent job pulling into a parking spot in front of a swanky hotel that looks like an oversized log cabin. Situated a little ways away from the water, it offers privacy from swimmers, but would still afford a grand view in the daylight. Already, my fingers itch to paint it.

Belly full, mind spinning with thoughts of going for a hike the next day to find the perfect location for preliminary sketches, I push through the front doors and step into the hotel lobby. Grand soaring beams frame the two-story high entrance. A fire crackles directly across from the front door, an ornate floor-to-ceiling stone fireplace. The warmth wafts over me in waves, warding off the lingering spring chill still stubbornly clinging to the air. Renee hadn't been kidding when she said the place is gorgeous. Well, when I asked where she'd recommend I stay for a while she'd said, "The Bear Lake Lodge is where you need to go. Don't even look at anywhere else. The owner? Ford Collier. Mmhmm is he something to look at. The place itself is almost as gorgeous as he is. If you want views, that's where you want to be."

I don't know about the gorgeous man, but she hadn't been wrong about the lodge. It is stunning. Almost worth the price tag I'd looked up online before the drive over. I gave a little mental shrug as I step up to the check-in desk off to my right. My little nest egg will take a punch, but if this place brought back the urge to paint, it'd be worth its weight in gold.

The space behind the desk was empty, so I ring the little silver bell on the counter and turn to wait. I can't get over how cozy and warm the place feels. Thick braided rugs are strategically placed throughout the common areas on the first floor, which features an open-concept floor plan. But the real stunner is the sweeping expanse of windows on either side of the gigantic fireplace. The first thing I'm going to do in the morning is get a mug of coffee from the complimentary bar and sit in the big, fluffy chair in front of those windows. I can't see out them now because it's too dark, only dots of lights from other cabins and the faintest hint of navy blue water are visible, but I know come morning the view will be awe-inspiring.

"Can I help you?" comes a gruff voice at my back. I jump and swirl around at the same time, knocking my elbow on the corner of the countertop and biting back a stream of curses.

I bite my cheek to keep from swallowing my tongue.

Renee hadn't been wrong about the owner either, it seems.

THE WILLOWY BLONDE isn't as collected as her fancy clothes and designer purse make her seem. Her pretty bronzed complexion goes stark white, then red as her deep blue eyes land on me. I say nothing in response to her reaction. All I want is to get her checked in and settled, then go back to my room with a beer and a baseball game on low.

"I'm sorry," she says when she catches her breath. She bites her lower lip, the tip of her pink tongue darting out to wet it. "I didn't hear you coming."

Why is it they always have to chit-chat? This is exactly why I have Nell on the front desk. I have neither the time or the patience to deal with the customer part of "customer service". "Need a room?"

Her hands tremble as she sets her Michael Kors bag on the counter with a clunk and digs through it. Silver rings glitter on slim, nimble fingers, flashing like lightning bugs. Her trim, unpainted nails have multi colored specks, a rainbow of color. Mildly amused, I wonder if it's another one of those weird nail trends women seem to like that I sure as hell don't understand.

"Yes, please," she says with a glance under her hooded eyes. "For the week? With the possibility of extending."

"Weekly rate is five hundred."

She doesn't bat an eye as she pulls out a credit card. "That'll be fine, thank you."

I grunt in response as I consult the computer. "I've got a double on the second floor with a view of the lake available."

"That's perfect."

I don't happen to think so. The last thing I need is a pretty blonde with secrets in her eyes busting up in my peace and quiet, but I keep my mouth shut and take her card and book the room.

She doesn't make idle chatter, which I grudgingly appreciate. Instead, she seems content to study the lobby, especially the windows. I'd be lying if I said I wasn't proud of the place. It wasn't a firefight in Afghanistan, but it kept my hands—and my mind—busy, which was more than I could say for a lot of the men I served with. Definitely more than I deserved.

I pass over the key cards to her room and a brochure

with local attractions, lodge amenities and a map. "Your room is just up the staircase to the right. Number 202. We're zero on the phone if you have any trouble."

"Thank you," she says and hefts her purse over her shoulder. "Have a good night Mr. ..."

I clear my throat. Another reason why I liked to stay in the back. It was a surefire way to keep from being on the receiving end of the curiosity that inevitably came from giving my name. "Ford, Ford Collier."

"Mr. Collier." Her bright smile disarms me. Either she's a real good actress or she had to have been hiding under a rock for the past couple years. I give a mental shrug. "Just Ford."

"Ford," she repeats softly. "I'm Peyton Rhodes. It's nice to meet you."

I take her offered hand and shake, frowning at the blue splotch of paint on her wrist. The single note of disarray contradicts her fancy purse and glittering adornments. It makes me frown. So it wasn't a fashion choice. I don't want to know where she got it from, but I do. "You, too," I say gruffly.

With another smile in my direction, she disappears up the staircase to her room and even though I tell myself not to, I stare at her ass the whole way up.

Somehow reminding myself that women like her are

nothing but trouble doesn't do a damn thing to get me to look away.

The next morning before I've even had my first cup of coffee—if you could call it that—Peyton comes downstairs and, with a small, polite smile in my direction, heads to the bar where we set out a little breakfast with coffee that doesn't taste like the sludge I make. I try not to look at her, but my eyes have other ideas. The tight black pants she somehow slicked herself into showcase stunner legs even a monk like me can appreciate.

"Good morning," she says.

I nod to her and busy myself on the computer, but I keep watch on her out of the corner of my eye. After she fills a cup and adds a shit ton of cream and sugar, she takes it with her and goes over to one of the lounge chairs in front of the window. I took her more for the excursions and Instagram type, but she stays there, sipping her coffee and watching the world outside the window come to life as the sun rises over ancient oaks.

The crooning voice of George Strait filtered in from the office, causing me to scowl. Nell, a sixty-five-year-old Windy Point native, listens to the local country radio station every day without fail. And each day I threaten to fire her because of it.

So far, she hasn't taken me seriously.

"How many times do I have to tell you to turn that shit off?" I ask when she pushes through the swinging door from the back office.

Nell, a Paula Dean twin if there ever was one, smiles silkily. Her glossy silver-white hair doesn't have a strand out of place. Much like the woman herself, she's as neat as a pin and militant about detail. My drill sergeant would have loved her.

"Well, honey, you can ask until we're both stone cold in our graves, but the answer is still going to be no."

"I really ought to fire you."

Nell lifts a hand to my cheek and pats it smartly as I shy away. She outdoes Peyton when it comes to the number of rings on her fingers. "You can sure try. I worked here before you were born and I'll probably be here long after you're gone."

I snort. "I'm not going anywhere, Nell."

Her lips, painted a pale pink, pull into a smile. "Then you'd better get used it, then, haven't you?"

"I really ought to fire you," I repeat to her back.

Nell pours herself a cup of coffee and says a cheerful "Good morning" to Peyton, who beams sunnily back at her. That pretty, easy smile pulls at me in ways that I don't like. But it's more than the smile. It's that I want it directed at me, which is a complication I sure as hell don't want or need.

We don't get many visitors to Windy Point this time of year. Most tourists tend to prefer the summer months, when the weather is clear enough for a hike or swim. The name Rhodes wasn't familiar, so she doesn't have family here. Her clothes don't exactly paint her as a drifter and I'm not one to notice cuts or material. It makes me wonder what brought her to this town, to my lodge.

More specifically, it makes me want her to leave because I don't want to wonder.

I don't want to know any more about her than I already do.

It wouldn't take long for word to get around about her, the way small towns work and then I won't have a choice. I knew that from personal experience. The gossip hotline would have her life story before sunup the next morning, if it didn't already. In fact, now that I thought about it, I'm surprised Nell didn't come in with a file as thick as my arm.

Her silver eyebrows wiggle when she comes back to the counter.

"Got us a pretty one today. When was the last time you went on a date?"

My scowl deepens. This is exactly how gossip starts. "You're pushing it, Nell."

The multiple rings adorning her fingers click as she

24

types lighting speed on the computer, working whatever magic it is that keeps the lodge running smoothly. "Then I know I'm asking the right questions. People tend to get all riled up when someone pokes the spots they know are tender. Missing female company lately, boss?"

"At the current moment, I've got all the female company I can handle, thanks."

Nell harrumphs, then smiles triumphantly. "I'd say you do," she replies.

The hairs on the back of my neck stand up. Yep, this woman is definitely all kinds of trouble.

I used to be good at trouble, once upon a time.

Turning to the counter, I bathe my tongue in a combination of toxic sludge and lava and grunt as Peyton shifts from foot to foot.

"Hi. I was wondering if you could recommend a trail for a novice. Something that won't get me lost. Preferably one that leads up into the mountains, if possible."

I raise a brow, but pull out a pamphlet and mark a couple options with a pen. Pointing to the first, I say, "This one will lead you on a trek around the lake. Nothing much by way of views, but it's about impossible to get lost. The one to the north of the grounds will take you through some baby hills. The mountains are a bit of a hike, but if you leave now you should make it back by dinner time. That's this trail here."

Her perfectly arched brows pucker as she studies the trails I've indicated with crudely drawn marks on the map. Leaning over the counter the way she is, I can smell the expensive perfume she must have doused herself in. It's been two years since my last tour in Afghanistan, but I'm as celibate now as I was then.

"I think I'll take the mountain trip. Send help if I'm not back by dark," she jokes. When I don't answer, her face falls and she clears her throat. "Right, well, thank you for your help." After giving Nell a little wave, she adds, "Have a good morning!"

"Smooth," Nell comments from behind me. "You aren't gonna rectify getting a woman if your pickup skills are that rusty."

Turning to face her, I give her a mental shove to say one more smart-mouthed thing. It's not a normal day if I haven't fired her at least a dozen times before lunch. "That could be because I wasn't trying to pick her up."

Nell's eyes twinkle mischievously. "Sure. So that's why you couldn't stop staring at her. Well, at least you've got a second chance. She left her wallet."

Cursing under my breath, I snag the trendy, frilly thing off the counter and hurry to catch her before she disappears into the woods. By chance I see a flash of blonde hair out of the corner of my eye. I shout her name, but she's either in her own little word or doesn't want a damn thing to do with me. I wouldn't blame her.

"Peyton!"

When I get close, I tap her shoulder with a hand and she flies nearly a foot up in the air, whirling around, eyes wild.

"Whoa, there," I say and take a cautious step back. "It's just me."

Panicked, wheezing breaths heave out of her lungs. "Jesus, you can't sneak up on people like that."

She's got the wide, panicked eyes of someone afraid of death. I'd seen it enough in my own to recognize it in someone else. Who had hurt her? What had she been through to make her come to Nowhere, North Carolina? "Is everything okay?" The words are out of my mouth before I can stop them and I regret asking the second I see her hands clench by her sides.

The fear in her gaze hardens and whatever ghosts she was remembering disappear behind her narrowed eyes. She pulls a pair of earbuds out of her ears. "Of course. I'm sorry, I didn't hear you. Did you need something?"

I don't miss that she takes a step back as I get closer and it's a battle to keep myself from scowling automatically. In the years since I've been a civilian again, I'd gotten used to a variety of reactions. Hero-worship, disdain, disgust, but the one that really gets me is horror. If Peyton's shoulders get any closer to her ears, she's gonna create a spontaneous black hole and swallow herself. Her peaches and cream skin has gone ash-white. If I hadn't seen her the day before, I would have thought she was sick or something.

She flinches when I thrust her wallet in her direction and this time I don't bother holding back the scowl, which only makes her shrink into herself all the more. "You forgot this back at the lodge." If my tone comes out more harsh than I intend, I decide fuck it. Pretty little princess wants to play explorer, she's got worse things to worry about than a beaten down former Marine like me. I may look like a tank, but the last thing on my mind is hurting anyone—especially a woman. Whatever happened to her in the past isn't my fault.

It isn't my fault.

I avert my gaze, the rush of memories, regrets, too much to bear. When I open my mouth, I find it's gone dry, so I bite back the reminder for her to be careful.

She isn't my responsibility. She can barely look at me without wincing. Maybe I am the monster the media made me out to be.

With that thought and her frightened stare weighing down my shoulders, I turn on my feet and stalk back to the lodge.

CHAPTER THREE
PEYTON

For many months, I was a prisoner in my own home.

You'd think it couldn't get worse than that, but it can. When I did venture out into the world again, it was with the fearful innocence of a child.

Except I didn't have any parents' legs to cling to, to turn to for comfort. All I had was myself and the nightmares that haunted me.

As I hike through the forest, the early morning sun blotted out by the thick canopy of trees, the cold fingertips of fear grip my heart as though no time has passed between that night and the present. All the work I'd done, all the physical space and time had gone the instant he caught me off guard. My blood still pounds like a metronome on speed in my ears.

"Stupid, stupid, stupid," I mutter to myself, kicking at

pine needles littering the forest floor and dusting up the air with the scent of still-cold earth.

It took me a long time after that night to even be around men I knew without having a panic attack, let alone strangers. Despite all the therapy, all my affirmations, and progress, big men like Ford still made me jittery. I had to tell myself to calm down and practice my breathing in order to remind myself not all men are bad guys. Not all men want to hurt me.

Once Ford stalks off back to the lodge it takes longer than I want to admit for the panic to fade. I don't want to blame him specifically. Even if it had been the nicest guy in the world, having someone come up behind me would have freaked me out.

Ford Collier, from his shit kicker boots to his permanent resting bitch face is no nice guy, that's certain.

He could be on covers of magazines if it weren't for the permanent scowl.

And the terrible attitude.

What was it about being so good-looking that turned men into insufferable jerks?

It's not really him I'm annoyed with, if I'm being honest with myself. It's me. *Cut that out, Peyton.* I can't go down that line of thinking. Only a shame spiral with a dose of depression will be the result, so I focus on the scenery around me, trying to lose myself in the scents and sounds.

I stomp through the trees with more energy than I've had in months, but it still takes me over an hour to get deep into the low rise of the mountains. Since it's my first time, I didn't pack the bulkier of my supplies. I figured I'd save that for my trip to the fabled Windy Point where the views were lauded by the brochures to be even more spectacular. I'd be able to bring my paints along then, maybe an easel and a larger canvas.

Some artists take photos of the landscape and compose in their studios, but for now on location will do. Not only do I not have a studio to speak of at the moment, but I've spent so much time locked up behind walls, staying indoors is the last thing I want to do.

A bird trills and then a flash of white darts in front of my vision to take roost at the top of the trees. I refocus on my surroundings, pushing the interaction with Ford to the farthest reaches of my mind. I'll apologize when I get back to the lodge. It's not his fault I'm so damaged.

My cell rings in the pocket of my backpack and I curse underneath my breath as it breaks my tentative serene mood. The display reads *Uncle Brad*.

"I'm alive," I say immediately.

Uncle Brad doesn't respond with his customary snort. Instead, he says, "Went to your place. The landlady told me you'd sublet it."

"Everything is fine," I say automatically. "I just...needed

to get away for awhile. I promise I'm okay. You don't need to worry."

Uncle Brad is—was—my mother's brother. After she passed, his incredibly overprotective instincts transferred to me like some sort of wacky familial inheritance.

"Without telling me," he says. I wince, grateful he can't see me.

"I knew you would have talked me out of it."

His sigh fills my ears over the line. I can picture him at the desk in his study, his glasses hooked on the vee of his shirt, a snifter of whiskey at his elbow and the bottle never far away. I'd conquered my demons...mostly. Uncle Brad had a harder time with his.

"Am I really that bad?" His soft question makes me pause more than a sharply worded admonishment would.

I pause the trek up the path and wipe at the sweat dripping down my brow and take a drink of water. The interruption helps me gather my thoughts.

"Of course not, Uncle Brad. I just, I could feel myself dying there. I knew if I didn't leave that house, that town, I'd never get out again. Please don't be mad."

"You know I'm just looking out for you, peanut." I'm not sure, but I swear I can hear his voice thicken. In the years since I lost my parents, I rarely saw evidence of his own grief so knowing I hurt him tears me up inside.

My nose stings as I tear up in turn. I blink my eyes

rapidly to keep the tears from spilling over. "I know you are, but you don't need to worry. I'm staying at a really nice hotel, I'm not sure how long, maybe a week or so. It's so gorgeous here. I'm actually on my way up one of the mountains to paint."

"No shit?" he asks and I can tell my admission stuns him.

"No shit. I decided just to drive for a while to see if anything moved me and this place, the views. I had to paint them the moment I saw them."

"That's wonderful, Peyton." He pauses, then adds, "I'm sorry if I came on too strong."

I begin walking and with each step, the bands around my chest loosens. The sun warms my chilled skin. Nothing can hurt me here. "You worry too much, Uncle Brad."

But he has good reason to worry. A long time ago, the decisions I made affected us both.

"I think I worry just enough. You going to tell me where you ended up or do I need to take more drastic measures?"

"North Carolina. A town called Windy Point." It makes me smile to hear the sound of fingers tapping against a keyboard. He may be overprotective, but he's mine. No doubt he's already searching the hell out of the little town. It wouldn't surprise me if he had a detailed report within twenty-four hours. My uncle may have been a nerdy professor, but he was an efficient one.

"Are you safe?"

I think of Ford and grimace a little. He is *definitely* not what I would classify as safe.

"This town is a regular *Pleasantville*, Uncle Brad. You know, before it turned technicolor. Nothing is going to happen to me here. You can relax."

"You know I just want what's best for you sweetheart."

I nod, even though he can't see me. "Of course I do. I promise you don't have anything to worry about while I'm here."

"Are you planning to go somewhere else after?"

The hill crests and I pause to study the view. What little breath I have after the climb releases from my chest in a whoosh. I'm not the type of person who believes in fate or whatever, but looking out over the trees, seeing Bear Lake in the distance feels a lot like it.

"I'm not sure," I say, answering his question. "But I have a feeling I'm going to like it here."

"You'll make sure to lock the doors right?" We both know a locked door won't stop a determined psychopath, but it makes him feel better to say it, so I let him.

"It's a hotel, not the ghetto, but I will, I promise."

"Take care, peanut."

"You, too."

I MADE IT BACK TO THE LODGE JUST BEFORE NIGHTFALL. The trail may have been a bit too much for an amateur like me, but it had been worth it. Something about being outside soothed me when it had terrified me just a short time ago. Repeating it helped to make it true. I'd never quite be comfortable in my own skin again, but process was to be celebrated. Being outside, alone, vulnerable. That was major progress for me.

Maybe when I got up to my room I'd order room service. Something decadent to celebrate. A good meal with wine and a hot bath sounds heavenly. I deserve a special treat for completing my first painting in months. It wouldn't win any awards and it certainly isn't my best piece, but putting brush to canvas again was like breathing for the first time in years. The catharsis was worth all the aches and pains.

The straps of the backpack dig into my shoulders. My thighs and calves scream with each step. I pull open the front door and a wave of warm air from the lit fire in the massive fireplace hits me, making more sweat pop out under my arms and between my breasts. A shower. All I want is a shower. Then the food and wine.

One person, a woman in a tight red dress that seems a little out of place for a town like Windy Point, leans over the front desk talking to Ford. From her body language, I'd gotten good at watching people over the time I'd spent too afraid to go outside and interact with them, tells me she's clearly in seduction mode. Ford, being seduced. I almost snort.

I'm on the bottom step of the grand staircase when her voice turns shrill. Even though I don't want to be involved in whatever scene she's trying to orchestrate, I can't help but turn around. Maybe because a little part of me wants to see Ford knocked down a peg or two. Then, I recognize her--the bombshell from the diner.

"You can't tell me no. My family practically runs this town. We need your meeting space for the small business owner's meeting this weekend."

There's another couple sitting near the fire, but their intimate conversation halts at the banshee's shrieks.

From my place across the hall, I can't hear Ford's response, but I can imagine, vividly, what effect threats have on a man like him.

The woman pushes away from the counter. "This is ridiculous. My father will hear about this."

Now that she's moved back a half-step, I can see Ford behind the counter. He doesn't look as threatening and as intimidating as a charging bull like he had a couple hours before. In fact, he looks completely blank, almost calm. He catches my eyes, holds my gaze for a half second, just long enough for heat to rise up the column of my throat.

I turn away and remind myself to apologize. Later. I

definitely don't want to do it in front of the woman determined to make a scene. I don't want to do it at all and have already made my mind up that I want to spend as little time with Ford as possible.

He's too big. Too intimidating. Too...dangerous.

I may be trying to get back out in the world and test my limits, but Ford isn't a test I'm willing to take.

"You should be grateful I'm even willing to do business here," I hear the woman say over my shoulder as I reach the top of the stairs. "Considering your reputation," she adds before gliding out the door.

My head turns involuntarily, curiosity overwhelming common sense, but Ford isn't behind the desk or anywhere in sight from my vantage point. Shaking my head, I insert the key into the slot and step into my room.

It takes a moment for me to realize I'm surrounded by shadows and my heart thuds in my chest. Frozen by fear in the entryway, I almost can't force myself to take another step inside. Only by telling myself there's nothing to be afraid of am I able to take the remaining steps forward.

I dump my backpack on the chair by the dresser and click on a lamp to dispel the darkness. I thought I'd left it on before my trek, but I must have forgotten. Not like me, considering in addition to my other phobias, I have an intense fear of the dark, especially being trapped in dark places.

Striding to the bathroom to confront whatever ghosts may lurk, I tell myself to stop being silly. It's a new place and that's why I feel unsettled. I repeat the affirmations given to me by my therapist and start the hot water running for the bath.

When I order dinner a few minutes later, I ask for the whole bottle of wine.

CHAPTER FOUR
FORD

THE NEXT DAY, I open the employee-only door to find something worse than a spoiled princess waiting for me on the other side. I'd rather face a porch full of socialites armed to the teeth than my baby sister Mercedes.

As if things couldn't get any worse.

"Now's not a good time, Mercedes." My parents thought they were clever naming their kids after vehicles. According to them, we were lacking in a sense of humor when we didn't find it as funny. I just thank God they didn't name me Volkswagen instead of Ford.

"It's never a good time with you," she says, then adds, "Don't call me Mercedes." But I can't help it. I've bugged her about her name since we were kids and I don't expect that'll change anytime soon.

"Hi, Lexie," I say to my niece, who's standing behind her mother working on a champion sulk.

Thankfully, my sister curbed her desire to continue the Collier christening tradition enough to name Alexus instead of Lexus. She nods to me then goes back to texting or chatting or whatever the thirteen-year-old girls are doing these days.

Mercy shifts and I notice the large duffle bag she has slung over one shoulder. "It won't be for long."

I scrub a hand absently over my hair and roll my shoulders. "I wasn't kidding when I said this isn't a good time. We're nearly fully booked. Can't you stay at mom and dad's?"

Mercy purses her lips and then Lexie adds, "We already asked them," causing Mercy to glare.

At my look Mercy explains, "They're going on a trip to see some lighthouses up north or whatever and having the floors in the house ripped up and replaced while they're gone. Please, Ford. Don't make me beg."

Lexie can't look me in the face at the pleading tone in her mother's voice and it causes me to relent. "Of course you can stay if you don't mind sharing the spare room in my quarters. It's not fancy," I warn.

Mercy perks up. "No that's fine. I promise, you'll hardly even know I'm here. We promise."

I snort as I hold the door open for them to come in. "That's what you said last time."

"The waterbed wasn't my fault," Mercy says. "How was I supposed to know it would rip?"

"I lost my deposit over the mess you made, I hope you know."

They throw their bags in the last room down the hall and we all take a seat on the couches in front of the t.v. and I have to admit, I hadn't realized how lonely my part of the lodge had been until their senseless chatter fills the silence.

"Ugh, mom," Lexie rolls her eyes and takes the controller to change the movie I had on. "I really don't want to hear about your sex life."

"Me either," I say.

"The both of you can shut your cake-holes. It was an accident. And Lexie, I don't ever want to hear you say the word sex again."

"Sex, sex, sex," Lexie retorts and sticks out her tongue.

Lexie's foot is within reach, so I grab hold of her ankle and yank her across the length of the leather couch and dig my fingers into her ribs. She shrieks and bats her hands at me, but I subdue them with my free arm.

"Who's your favorite uncle?" I ask her.

Her face turns red with the force of her laughter. "Stop, omigod. You s-suck."

Her screams make my ears ring, but they also pull me

out of the funk I'd been in ever since I woke up after a nightmare with Peyton's terrified face lodged firmly in my memories. I don't know what trouble my sister's found herself in, but I'll take it in exchange for this.

"I give," she says after a few more minutes. "Fine, I won't say it again."

"Promise," I ask.

She draws in deep gulps of air, her long, dark hair askew. "I promise."

Mercy jumps to her feet and rushes to the door the moment a knock sounds. "I'll get it," she says. I don't miss the tell-tale way she fluffs her hair or the slight tremor of excitement in her voice.

"Expecting someone?" I ask as I sit up straight. There's no way she could have called someone to come over. She'd barely been here a half hour. If I know Mercy, and sometimes even though it shames me to admit it, I wish I didn't, she'd told her new flavor of the week to meet her at my place because here she has a built-in babysitter. I may say no to Mercy, but we both know I'll never say no when it comes to my niece.

Lexie keeps her eyes squarely on the t.v. as her mother snatches the door open so quickly I fear for the hinges. "You made it," she says to the person on the other side.

"You know I'd do anything for you, sugar," comes the responding male voice.

A part of me wonders what she would have done if I *had* told her about my troubles, about the debilitating injury, the nightmares. But it had been a long time since I confided anything to her. Not that she didn't try. After my first deployment, she made it a point to come by and talk, but at the time I just wasn't interested. Sometimes talking about things makes them all the more real. And there are some experiences I don't need to be more realistic. There are enough complications from the hell I've endured—I don't need to add a pissed off Mercy to them.

"Ready to go?" the guy asks.

Mercy glances at me from around the door and I just wave to her. I don't have the energy to argue and Lexie and I will probably have more fun by ourselves as it is.

Mercy squeals and grabs her purse. "It'll just be a couple hours, I promise."

"Yeah, right," Lexie says under her breath.

The door shuts behind them, cutting off Mercy's exuberant laughter. I hear the revving of a motor and then the squeal of tires and spitting of gravel. I shake my head a little. Some things never change.

"THAT WAS..."

"Disgusting?" I supply.

Lexie laughs. "Unappetizing," she counters.

"I'm sorry, kiddo. I'll order pizza. Apparently, I haven't gotten any better at cooking the last year since I've seen you."

"I told you that you should have let me cook."

"Noted. Next time, you're the chef. Grab my phone and order some, would you? My card info is already saved on the app."

"You're hopeless," she says.

"Hopelessly awesome," I call out after her.

It's been a couple hours since Mercy left, but Lexie doesn't seem to notice. Or at least, she tries pretty hard to make it look that way. I did my level best to distract her with a couple movies and a relentless stream of teasing. Accompanied with the horror shot that is dinner, I think I did alright.

The meatloaf I'd attempted to make was probably the low point, I decide as I scrape what's left of the charred block into the garbage can. Not my fault. Most of my food my adult life came ready-to-eat so I can't be held responsible when I'm put in charge of making it.

Another knock comes at the door as I'm elbow-deep in suds trying to scrape the congealed disaster off the pan. "Can you get that?" I call out to Lexie. I'm not technically working today, but as the owner of one of the most prominent tourist locales in the town of Windy Point, I'm always working.

I hear the door open and the low chatter of the delivery guy followed by Lexie's response. Stomach growling, I think screw the dishes and leave the whole lot of them to soak in the sink. I'll worry about them later.

Lexie's still at the door when I get to the living room. She's juggling two large pizza boxes and a package from some mail delivery service on top of that.

"Need some help with that?" I ask, but her response is interrupted by the familiar sound of an engine revving.

I look past Lexie in the doorway and see a douched-up Ford Mustang in my driveway. Mercy's in the front seat. At first, I try to pull Lexie back inside. No one should have to see their mother MILF-ing it up with some prick. Then, Mercy jerks back, but not because of anything good.

The motherfucker hit her.

A surge of adrenaline propels me to maneuver Lexie back inside with one hand. I don't know how I manage to do it without dumping everything in her hands on the sidewalk, but I do. My long strides eat up the distance between the front door and the car in seconds. I see Peyton out of the corner of my eye, but I don't have time to worry about her. In another few steps, I throw open the door with one hand and yank Mercy out with the other.

She screeches like a pissed off alley-cat and I shove her in the direction of the lodge. "Get inside," I tell her without looking at her.

"I can handle it, Ford," she protests and tries to force her way between me and the car, but that's not happening.

I turn and pin her with a glare. "Go inside with your daughter," I say slowly.

The mention of Lexie has Mercy pausing long enough for me to scoot her a couple more feet in that direction. She sees Lexie peering out from behind the curtains and whatever maternal instincts she must have pull her toward the lodge. Peyton gives the scene one last glance, then scurries back around to the front entrance.

Putting her out of my mind, I turn back to the dude in the car and see he's as much of a douche as his ride. "Don't come back," I tell him.

"Or what? Gonna kill me, too?"

"What'd he say?" Mercy screeches.

I lift a hand and gesture for her to get her ass inside. To the douche, I say, "You wanna try me and find out?"

He considers it for all of two seconds before he puts the car in reverse.

"Smart choice," I tell him and slam the door.

I watch as he speeds out of the driveway until I can no longer see him.

Mercy is waiting for me as soon as I go back in the house.

"I'm so sorry," she says. Her makeup is smeared and her

eyes are watery. The redness around her eyes is already starting to darken.

Adrenaline still pulses in my veins. It worries me more than a little how much I missed this feeling. "It's fine, it's fine. Next time don't bring assholes like that around my place, though, Merc." I glance at Lexie, whose hovering in the doorway that leads to the kitchen.

"I won't, I promise," Mercy says and then wraps her arm around her daughter. They both go into the kitchen as I close up the front door.

I couldn't protect my men, but I damn sure won't let anything happen to the people I care about.

CHAPTER FIVE
PEYTON

THE WATER IS COLD, too cold, assuredly, for me to be dipping my feet in it just yet, but I can't help myself. The freezing temperature grounds me and I concentrate on noting the sensations in my body that root me in reality.

My toes dig into the grainy texture of the sand until both feet are buried completely beneath the surface. With my eyes closed the sounds, scents and feel of the world around me is amplified. It's a technique I learned in therapy to take my mind out of the realm of panic and toward calm.

I chickened out of apologizing for snapping at him after seeing Ford in another confrontation with another woman and some guy in a tricked out car. I could tell from the look in his eye he was in no mood for interference, so I kept my distance and instead trekked around the lake and enjoyed another meal in my room. Nightmares plagued my sleep and I woke up covered in a cold sweat with my heart still racing from an invisible attacker.

The thought occurred to me to stay in my room for the day, give myself a break from the over-stimulation, but I knew if I stayed it would be one more step toward holing myself up behind the security of a lock and never coming out again. I forced myself to get out of bed, dress, and speed-walked blindly out of the lodge and found myself at the lake.

My heart began to settle and my breathing to quiet as I focus on the lap of the cool water against my ankles. In the distance, I hear the muted rumble of a lawn mower roar to life, followed by the sharp scent of freshly cut grass. Rooting myself in the present is one of the only sure ways I know to keep from being swallowed by the past.

"That wasn't what it looked like, yesterday."

I keep my eyes closed, thankful I didn't jump and screech like a frightened little rabbit this time. "None of my business."

"I don't want you think I go around terrorizing the locals," he says, his gruff voice sounding closer than before.

"Why would it matter what I think?" I ask and finally turn to peer up at him, having to smother the instantaneous instinct to put a safe distance between us.

He's too tall to be human. His shoulders look like he's

packing some serious muscles underneath the t-shirt and flannel button up he's sporting. As he studies me in turn, I wonder what he does in spare time to be so built, chop down trees? Certainly the tingling in my stomach isn't... attraction. It's nerves. There's no way in hell I could want a man like Ford, a brutal beast capable of violence.

"It doesn't." I nearly roll my eyes at his bluntness. So much for my feelings. "But you're a guest. I don't want you to be uncomfortable while you're here and we seem to have gotten off on the wrong foot." The words are robotic, mechanical. I wonder if he's given this speech before.

"Thank you for your concern, but I'm fine." My own response is just as mechanical. Maybe Ford and I have more in common than I'm willing to admit.

He rolls his massive shoulders, squinting against the rising sun. "None of my business. You're not from around here, are you?"

"I thought you said it wasn't any of your business?"

"Just making conversation."

Silver glints in the light at his neck. The beaded chain is a familiar one—military dog-tags, which makes a lot of details click into place. His careful, watchful nature. The intensity of his stare. His physique. Even the hardness around his eyes and mouth. He'd seen violence, caused it.

Death, I'd learned, stained people once they came in

contact with it. It settles over your shoulders like a mantle you can't ever take off.

Whose death was on his?

Long seconds pass and I realize he's staring at me as I stare at him. My cheeks burn. "No, I'm not from around here."

"Vacation?"

"Sort of. What about you?" I turn and sit on the dock, watching him as I cross my legs and try to relax in his commanding presence. Sitting down only causes him to tower over me, but it hides the fact that even though I know he won't hurt me he causes my legs to shake.

"My parents used to own the place. When they decided to retire, I took over."

I don't know why, but those last words make me shiver. "You were in the military before then?"

Must be a sore subject because his lips thin. "Marines. Ten years."

"My dad was in the Navy. Desk jobs, mostly."

This causes him to turn that laser gaze to me. "You were a military brat?"

"Sort of. He retired before I was born. I was a surprise baby, my parents didn't think they could get pregnant. You?"

He winces. "I wish I was an only child. Older sister, Mercedes. You saw her and her daughter, Lexie, yesterday."

So that wasn't his girlfriend. Doesn't matter. "I bet you drove each other crazy."

"I guess," he replies. Then he glances back to the lodge. "I'd better get back. You okay out here?"

I hate that question. "I'm *fine*."

He looks like he wants to say something else, but he just shrugs. I watch him walking back up the trail for far, far too long for someone who isn't attracted to him at all.

To keep the promise to myself to get out of the room—and to stay away from Ford and the jittery feelings he gives me—I make the short drive into the heart of Windy Point. I park at a public parking lot next to the main street run of stores and shops, intent on passing time peeking through like a proper tourist, then stopping at one of the restaurants for lunch before I head back to the lodge to paint some more.

I stop first at a kitschy little trinket shop, the kind where they sell homemade jams and jellies along with local artisan crafts. I can't resist the blackberry jam and chocolate covered crickets and a darling bee carved from oak. Weighted down with my purchases, I move along to the next shop, a tea emporium. Loving the thought of sipping tea in the morning on the back deck at the lodge, I eagerly peruse their selection and add a sachet of blueberry green tea to my bag, already looking forward to brewing it.

The next shop makes my heart sing the moment I spot the sign. Splatters Studio is framed by blotches of colorful paint. It's a far cry from the high brow art scene I used to participate in, but that doesn't stop me from pushing through the bright red door. Some sort of lesson or group activity is taking place and I keep to the back of the main room so I don't interrupt.

A tall, statuesque woman leads the demonstration with a commanding presence. I observe in envy of her self-confidence, wondering what it must be like to be so sure of one's self. I'd been like that once. Maybe, with time in places like Windy Point, I'd find the girl I used to be.

It must be some sort of spin on a wine and paint night, except with pottery. The small group of women are each separated into pairs with lumps of clay in front of them and a variety of mixed drinks and glasses of wine at their elbows. Feminine chatter and laughter punctuates the woman's instructions.

I browse around the public front of the shop, noting the different services offered. Birthday parties with little pails of art supplies for party favors. Variations of tonight with different mediums and meeting times. More serious instruction for the dedicated hobbyists.

"Hello, I don't believe we've met before, I'm Alice Kent."

Turning from the display, I find the instructor standing behind me and am stunned silent because she's even more striking up close. In her mid-fifties or so, with thick framed glasses and dramatic silver hair, she towers at least half a foot over me.

I remember social niceties long enough to shake her hand. "Peyton. I'm sorry, I hope I didn't interrupt," I add with a glance back toward the group of women, who are now shuffling out of the space with the remnants of their drinks, their cheeks flushed with laughter and alcohol.

She smiles gently and adjusts her glasses. "No, of course not. We're always happy to have fresh blood here. New to the area or just visiting?"

I clutch the small bag of purchases in front of me. "A little bit of both."

"Ah, well why don't you stay for a little while to see what we're all about? I never say no to free labor," she says. "Are you into art?"

"That's like asking if I breathe." She hands me the mangled remains of molding clay on a tray and I follow behind her as she loads the rest into my arms.

"What mediums?"

"Anything really, though I stick mostly to canvas work."

Once we've cleared away the clay, Alice leads me

through a door that reads *Employee's Only* and we dump the supplies on a counter. She begins sorting through them and organizing them into their respective places.

"You should take one of my classes sometime," she offers. "Or if you're looking to stay longer, I can always use some help around here. Most of my part time work doesn't come in until the season starts. My husband and I are trying to prep to foster a child so sometimes I can be a bit short handed."

Wow, so this is what people meant when they said small towns can be friendly.

"I'm not sure exactly how long I'm planning to stay, but if it becomes more of a permanent situation, I'll definitely stop by."

I leave ten minutes later with her business card in my hand and the prospect of a future dancing around in my head. A future—that's what violent acts steal from you in addition to the scars they leave on your body or the people they wipe out from your lives. The future you planned for so long, coveted and nurtured. Mourning loved ones makes sense, but mourning the life you'll never get to have again? That's a mind trip.

Sensing my mind going down a path best left alone, I hurry down the street back toward my car. My shopping bag slaps repeatedly against my side. The farther I go, though, the more I feel the weight of someone watching me.

I brush it off, knowing I have a tendency to be hyper-sensitive and somewhat paranoid.

On my way back to the lodge, I swing by a drive-through and get a mound of tacos and a slushie. I plan to take my haul back to my room and lock myself in for a few hours of work. Alice's offer keeps rolling around in my mind as I navigate the winding roads.

What if I did decide to stick around for a while?

Windy Point, the mysterious Ford aside, is the first place I've felt comfortable and creative. Why not stay while I was feeling inspired? The moment I felt the itch to move on, nothing was keeping me here. I can move on until I want to stop or just keep playing gypsy for the rest of my life.

The reminder that I'm not trapped, that I'm free to make my own decisions calms me as I pull to a stop at the lodge. I didn't realize how much time has passed until I get out of the car and see the hazy moonlight glittering off the slices of lake visible between the thick tree trunks.

I pause by my open door and figure, screw it. Ford had interrupted me earlier, but the likelihood that will happen twice in a row is slim to none. Besides, the nerves clamoring in my stomach make me even more determined to go see the moon glimmering on the water. I'd been trapped by my mind for so long, I won't let myself be afraid of the dark anymore.

Leaving my purchases in the front seat, I lock my car and stride determinedly around the lodge on a stone path. My heart thunders in my ears and I feel cold and hot at the same time, but I force one foot in front of the other. All my instincts are screaming at me to turn around and go back to the lodge where the light shines from the dazzling windows like a beacon of hope, but I turn my back on them defiantly.

There's enough daylight left for me to walk without tripping over my own feet, but it makes visibility past about ten feet questionable at best. The shadows seem to whisper to me and each crackle from deep in the forest at either side or brush of wind along the naked branches has my pulse skittering.

A boat that skims the surface of the water in the distance eases my anxiety, if only a little. I'm not alone.

You're being silly, Peyton.

I chuckle a little at myself and slip out of my shoes as I reach the dock where I'd seen Ford earlier. He's nowhere in sight, so I relax and amble down the worn wood planks barefoot.

It isn't dark enough for stars to be visible, but the cloudless sky is a deep, unblemished blue. The jet black shapes of bats dart out from the trees above me and I watch as they swoop and dive feeding on the insects above. Tears spring to my eyes. My dad and I used to sit on our back porch swing and watch the bats come out at night. We'd talk about everything, silly conversations, really and he was probably nice and buzzed from an after-work beer. Those are the things I miss the most about my parents. The out-of-the-blue meaningless memories we shared. Inconsequential things we'll never get to do together again.

I groan, annoyed with myself, and brush the tears away. My eyes roam over the landscape, looking for a distraction and they go back to the boat. There's a couple on board and they're just close enough that I can see that they're having some sort of intimate conversation standing at the back of the boat. I shouldn't be watching them, but I'd gotten used to observing people the year I spent locked away in my house. It's a hard habit to break.

I can't make out anything other than their general shapes, but they're both sitting in the back seats of the boat, gesticulating wildly. Telling some sort of wild story, I imagine. I lean my cheek on my knees and let my thoughts drift as I watch them. With the sounds of the lake in the background, I nearly relax enough to forget how dark it's getting.

Then a shout breaks the silence.

I shoot to my feet and look on in horror as the figures begin to struggle. With the growing darkness, it's harder to see them, but there's no denying that they aren't having a calm conversation anymore. The man, who I think is dressed in jeans and towers over the other, shoots to their feet. The woman, dressed in a flowing sheath of some sort, takes a quick step back, trips, and goes down hard. I gasp aloud, but no one is close enough to hear me.

They're just arguing. It'll be over soon and you'll laugh it off. There's nothing to worry about.

The comfort of my hotel room beckons and I start to glance back to the safety of the lodge when a quick movement catches my eye. My feet freeze in place and my stomach rebels, clutching around emptiness and threatening to give my lunch a second appearance. The taller of the two shoves at the woman. The shadow of her flirty dress billows up as she falls back, hard, into the side of the boat.

"What the hell?" I whisper. Gone was the quiet, peaceful evening. The night that had been so comforting now pressed around me with renewed menace. "Talk it out. Apologize," I urge them. Except, the intimate conversation they seemed to have been having devolves into a screaming match. I can only hear the echoes of it and can't make out any of the words.

The woman tries to get up, but he shoves her back down and I wince, stomach churning, and all instincts screaming for me to flee. If not to get help, than to run and hide. Hiding is what I do best. But I can't. My knees are locked and I know if I leave I may not be able to help.

But there's no helping them.

The woman claws at the man holding her down and I

can tell from her high-pitched screams she's pleading even if I can't make out the words. Her voice rings in my ears until it's all I can hear. They blend with the memories of that night until I can't tell if what I'm hearing is the woman in front of me or the ghosts of my own nightmares.

"Stop, just stop. Shut up," I tell her, or them, I don't even know anymore. "You're going to piss him off." If she didn't, it's going to be bad.

It went from bad, to worse when the woman manages to get to her feet and charges at the man with her hands outstretched, nails no doubt gouging into any available flesh. The man backed away from her, toward my direction, then pivots until the woman went overboard.

I don't realize I'm shouting until I stop, thinking their argument is over once the woman hits the water. Maybe the freezing temperature will cool her off and they can have a rational discussion.

I nearly leave again, until the man kneels in the boat, to help her I assume at first. Then he stretches out his arms and all I can see is a violent thrashing in the water as the woman fights her way back to the surface.

"No!" I whisper before I realize what I'm doing.

All too soon, the water goes still.

For several long minutes, my terrified brain can't grasp what it means and then I understand all too well.

I trip over my own feet as I turn and try to sprint for the

lodge and fall into the black depths of Bear Lake, knocking my head on the dock as I go down.

I try to fight it, terror overtaking me at the thought of being helpless, but the darkness I tried so hard to overcome envelopes me.

CHAPTER SIX
FORD

"HAVE you seen Ms. Rhodes come in?" Nell asks the moment I walk in.

I glance up, wondering if she can see the tension in my face. "I just got back. How would I have seen her?"

Nell twists her hands looking too flustered to pay any attention to me. "I'm worried. Saw her go out back a while ago and she hasn't made it in yet. Do you think she wandered off and got herself lost in the woods?"

The coffee in my thermos has gone stone cold, but I choke it back anyway. I've had worse. "I think she's a grown woman and knows how to find her way back or call for help. I don't want to get involved. For Christ's sake I'm not her keeper." The look on Nell's face tells me she's not going to let this one go. "Fine, I'll go down to the lake trails and see if

I can find her, make sure she's okay. Will that make you feel better?"

Nell smiles and gives me a hug. "You're a good man, Ford."

I grunt as I get to my feet and throw on my jacket. "If you think that's true, you'll have another cup of coffee waiting for me when I get back."

"You got it," she says in a pleased voice to my retreating back.

With the flashlight I retrieve from under the front desk in my hand and my phone in the other, I head to the back deck, nodding to a couple sitting in front of the fire on my way. Cicadas hum around me as I head down the marked path from the back deck toward the lake. Damn silly woman would have had to work to get herself lost. The lodge is lit up light a Christmas tree at night for this very reason, but there's always some fool tourist who thinks they're master hikers who gets themselves lost.

The beam from the flashlight bobs in front of me as I dial the number Peyton provided when she checked in with my other hand. The line rings and rings until I get her voicemail. Peyton doesn't seem like the type to go anywhere without her phone attached to her side, so the first rumblings of unease stir inside me.

I pocket my phone and begin to search in earnest. The

trail to the water is empty and the top of Bear Lake is as smooth as glass.

Where the fuck could she be?

She probably went around to the front as I was going to the back or some other stupid crap. I tell myself that as I step out onto the dock, hoping I'll find her sitting at the end with her feet in the water again like I had this morning.

I find her alright, but she's face-down in the water with a murky halo of red that shimmers when I shine the light over her. *No!* I think, or maybe I shout it. My knees scream out in pain as I slam against the dock. The flashlight plummets from my nerveless hands and skitters away, the beam arching and twirling, flashing on Peyton in a sick carnival of lights.

Her skin is ice-cold by the time I wrap my hands around her arms and her lips are blue. Desperation has me pulling her out of the water with a roar, her limbs knocking against the wood like a rag doll's. I perform CPR, thankful for the combat medicine I learned in the Corps and hoping like hell it'll actually do me some good this time around.

Minutes pass like centuries with me working on her until she coughs, spitting up lake water and hacking for air. I brush back the hair from her face and rub her back until she settles. Her teeth chatter with the cold and I strip off my jacket and cover her with it.

"Peyton? Peyton it's Ford. Can you hear me?" Her eyes

flicker open and then focus on me. "That's it. Come back to me."

She blinks blearily. "W-what?"

"Wake up, sunshine. C'mon." She's cold. Far too cold and she won't stop shivering. I haul her against me, her body small and vulnerable against mine. The urge to protect, to save, is so overwhelming my grip tightens around her. She makes a sound of protest and I gentle my hold.

"Ford?" Her blue lips form my name, but no sound comes out. Her eyes roam over my face, confusion clouding them. "What?"

I brush my hand over her hair and it comes away red. Cursing, I pull a bandana from my pocket and press it to the knot on her head. She winces. "I'm sorry, you must have knocked your head good. You almost drowned."

"Drowned?" she repeats, shaking her head as though to clear her thoughts. Her eyebrows squish together and she blinks rapidly.

"Yeah, looks like you fell into the water and hit your head. If I hadn't found you, you could have drowned." Her eyes widen and she shoots up, nearly knocking heads with me. "What the hell, calm down. You could hurt yourself."

"He hurt her. She's hurt. We have to get help." She begins to struggle out of my arms like a wildcat.

"Hang on there, you keep steady now. You could make it worse." She rips out of my hold and stumbles back, nearly falling off the other end of the dock. "Peyton, what the hell?"

"He drowned her. He drowned her and we have to get help." Her eyes roll in her head and she flips onto her hands and knees and begins crawling when she can't get to her feet.

"Peyton, wait. Let me help you." She slaps my hands away when I try to help her stand. "Dammit, did that bump also knock all the common sense out of you? Calm down so we can fix this." I grab her by the arms and haul her up. When her knees buckle, I brace her against me. "You didn't drown. You're fine, you're here with me. You're safe."

Peyton grips my shirt with both fists. "Not me. God, not me. The woman on the boat. The man drowned her. I-I think she's dead. We have to help her."

I glance at the empty lake. "There's no one there, Peyton."

She spins around and I brace her wavering body with my arms. "What? No they were just there. A man and a woman, I think. They were arguing and he pushed her over and drowned her. I'm not making this up."

I guide her to the edge of the dock, picking up my flashlight along the way. When we get to the edge, I shine the beam out over the empty water. "Can you tell me what happened? Did you see who they were?"

She closes her eyes as she remembers. "I couldn't see

everything, they were pretty far across the lake, it was mostly just their shadows with the light of the moon behind them. I heard them arguing, once it got more intense, the sound of her falling after he shoved her nearly echoed. Then the splash of water when he pushed her over." When the shivers overtake her again, I wrap my jacket more securely around her shoulders.

I know what she's feeling. The sense of unreality, shock, disbelief. I never wanted to feel it again let alone watch someone else go through it right in front of me.

"Could you see what they were wearing?" I ask. "What the boat looked like? Maybe a tag or name?"

"Not really. The woman was in a dress, shorter than the man who had to be wearing pants, but that's about it. It was too dark," she ends on a whisper. She's shaking so violently, I worry she's in shock. "It's too dark. Can we go inside?"

As I walk her back up the dock, her body leaning into my side, I say, "Are you sure this is what you saw? Maybe you were mistaken. It's pretty hard to see a ways out, you could have been confused."

Her feet stop moving, forcing me to turn and look at her. Grief ravages her face and too late, I realize she's crying. She nods to the tags at my neck. "You were in the military, right? Would you mistake someone dying right in front of you?"

Point taken, we start walking again. "The boat. Can you describe it?"

She sighs. "I could probably pick one out if I saw it again. Big. I'm sorry, I'm tired."

We get to the edge of the dock and begin the short climb up the path that leads to the lodge.

"Why were you down at the lake?" I ask when she gets too quiet.

"Please, Ford. Don't interrogate me now. I'm too exhausted to argue."

My strides eat up the ground, but I have to pace myself to keep up with her. "I need to keep you focused and awake. Don't want you passing out on me. Tell me. Were you trying to take a midnight swim?"

"I'm an artist. I wanted to see what the water looked like at night." She rests her head against my shoulder and more of her weight leans against me. "It was so pretty."

I shake her awake. "Oh, no you don't. Wake up sleeping beauty."

She growls at me. "You're such an asshole, Ford."

I nearly smile. "Call me whatever you want, but you were underwater for God only knows how long. You hit your head and could be suffering from a concussion. Keeping you conscious supersedes being nice."

"I think I hate you," she says.

"You wouldn't be the first," I answer.

We reach the steps to the deck and she shoves out of my hold. "I can walk by myself."

She teeters a little at the top step, but manages to make it to the back door. A wave of heat greets us, along with Nell, and to my growing frustration, Mercy and Lexie.

"We, like, heard there was a missing woman," Lexie says in a whisper that carries. "Is that her?"

"Is everything okay?" Mercy asks.

"We'll talk later," I tell them. "Go to my rooms, please. Nell, will you call the sheriff?"

At the mention of the police, Peyton's face drains of all color. I cross to her in two long strides and catch her weight before she sinks to the ground.

"Oh sweet baby Jesus," Nell says as she hurries to the phone. For once in her life, she doesn't argue with me. Maybe I won't fire her today after all.

"Don't faint on me, sunshine."

She glares at me, her eyes clearing a bit. "I wasn't going to faint. I just got a little dizzy."

I walk her over to the seat in front of the fire. "Dizzy my ass, if I hadn't caught you, you'd be in a puddle on the floor, now snap out of it."

"You have a wonderful bedside manner," she hisses. "Has anyone ever told you that?"

Lifting her chin with my finger, I smile wanly. "You

don't look like you're gonna pass out now, so bedside manner or not, I got the job done."

She accepts a cup of coffee from Nell. "Thank you."

"Are you alright, honey?" Nell asks. "You had us worried."

Peyton doesn't answer. She doesn't really have to. The haunted look on her face is answer enough. To me, she says, "What were you doing out by the lake?" She tries to disguise it, but I note the wary tone in her voice.

Disappointment has my voice hardening and me taking a step back. I cross my arms over my chest. "I was looking for you. What else?"

"And you didn't see or hear anything?" she asks.

"Other than you floating face down in the water, no. I didn't really have time to pay attention to anything else, what with me saving your life and all."

The smile she gives me is fake and she doesn't look me directly in the eye. "Of course," she says, but it doesn't sound sincere.

I turn away from her and stalk to the front desk to wait for the police to arrive.

FORD HOVERS in the peripheral of my vision and even though I know it's foolish, I can't help but feel threatened. He saved me. I'd be dead if he hadn't found me. But that doesn't do anything for the survival instinct inside of me telling me to run away from him as fast as I can.

Men like Ford are dangerous. Not just because of what they're capable of physically, but because when I'm around him, it's so easy for me to forget my better judgement.

When I get to my feet, needing the space or just to move, it's like he's a satellite anchored to my position. He turns to me, his eyes watchful, waiting.

"I'm going to go get in some clean clothes," I announce. "I'll be back before the police get here."

"Of course," Nell says and I can tell she wants to hover, but she lets me go. She scurries to the counter and retrieves another keycard. I'd left mine with my purse and the bags of food and goodies in the car. "Here you go."

Grateful for the reprieve, even for just a moment, I hurry up to my room and close the door firmly behind me.

Keep yourself busy.

That's the only way I know to keep from dissolving into a sobbing mess, so I go to the clothes I neatly folded and put away in the dresser. I choose a pair of jeans and a soft cable knit sweater along with new underthings. My wet clothes land in a pile underneath the bathroom sink. I wish I could burn them, forget tonight and act like none of it ever happened, but I can't. My hair is a drenched, tangled mess, so I take the time to brush it out and pull it into a sleek ponytail.

The process of dressing and grooming calms me enough to face going back downstairs. A man in his mid-thirties in a dark brown uniform with a walkie at his shoulder and gun at his side stands at the front desk deep in conversation with Ford. The woman and child—Ford's family? I wonder— have disappeared. Nell is hovering about tidying the great room in a nervous habit that reminds me all too well of my own mom's tendency to clean when she was nervous.

Ford's eyes nearly pin me to the floor when he spots me at the foot of the stairs. "Sheriff Hadley, this is Peyton Rhodes, a guest here at the lodge. Peyton, this is Paul Hadley."

I hold out my hand, thankful it stopped shaking. "Sheriff," I say.

"Got somewhere private we can talk Collier?" the sheriff asks.

Ford studies me a moment longer, then jerks his head behind him. "Yeah, you can talk in the back. Nell, will you keep an eye on things out here?"

"Of course, boss." Nell sends me a sympathetic look.

Sheriff Paul Hadley isn't intimidating, per say. Around 5' 10" with dusty blonde hair desperately in need of a trim and watery blue eyes. When he turns to hold the door open for me, I'm close enough to see the dusting of freckles along the bridge of his nose. He's not quite as imposing as Ford, with less brawn and a more lackadaisical air. I've gotten good at judging people or at least getting an impression of them and Sheriff Hadley strikes me as an efficient man. The kind of guy you judge as affable at first until he proves himself to be more observant than you'd expect.

The room Ford's taken us to must be his office. It smells like him and I almost wish he'd brought me somewhere else. Being in a space where he spends so much of his time feels too intimate. The desk is what I guess could be described as organized chaos. Papers litter its surface in haphazard piles punctuated by pens and paper clips. It strikes me that there isn't a personal touch, no photographs or homemade knick knacks. No military service medals. I'd imagine he spends a lot of his time in here, but there's nothing personal adorning his desk. I wonder if he's trying to hide his past or if he's that much of a loner.

Ford offers me the big comfy chair behind his desk, but I shake my head and take one of the two guest chairs. The sheriff takes the other.

"Why don't you start at the beginning?" Sheriff Hadley suggests.

I knot my fingers in my lap and struggle for the right words. They tangle up in my throat and spill out over my lips. I try to relate all the details with as little emotion as possible, sticking to the relevant facts. As I talk, Ford goes to a little mini-fridge on a counter behind his desk and retrieves a couple bottles of water. He places one in front of me, then Sheriff Hadley. I pause speaking long enough to wet my throat. When I'm finished, the two men share a glance and silence settles over the room.

"So you didn't get a good look at either of them? Not enough to identify them?"

My head drops. "No, I'm sorry. They were too far away for me to get a good look at them."

Sheriff Hadley turns to Ford. "Where were you in all this? Did you see the assault, the murder, too?"

Ford shakes his head. "No, I came up after. I found Ms. Rhodes in the water. She'd hit her head and fell into the lake." He sips at his water and crosses his legs. "I didn't see anything on my way down. There were no boats on the water when I got there."

"What about the boat?" Hadley asks. "Did you see where it went, Ms. Rhodes, or where it came from?"

I take a sip of water. "No, it was already there when I got there and I didn't see which direction it went after."

The questioning. That's what I hate the most. I hated it before and now I hate it even more. The sly looks like they don't quite believe me. Having to prove myself, that I'm telling the truth. It causes bile to rise in the back of my throat.

"Could you tell whereabouts on the lake? Distance, direction?"

Closing my eyes, I try to remember where the boat had been. "From the dock it was at eleven o'clock, closer to the far side of the lake." I open my eyes and send them both an apologetic look. "I'm sorry I'm not of more help. It all happened so fast."

"Not like you could have turned into Superwoman and flew across the lake to save her." Ford sets his water on the table and says to Hadley, "I can take you in my boat if you want to give it a look now."

The sheriff nods and gets to his feet. "I appreciate it. Don't trouble yourself, Ms. Rhodes. We'll go take a look and see what we see. If you think of anything else, you let me know. Alright?"

"Sure. Yeah, I can do that."

Hadley takes the water bottle, sips, then readjusts his ball cap with a nod at Ford. My gaze follows him out the door until he disappears from sight.

"Why don't you head back up to your room?" Ford suggests. He stuffs keys and his cell phone into his pockets. That done, he crosses to a safe embedded in the wall and after putting in the code, he takes out a vicious looking handgun, which he loads and straps on with a shoulder holster. "This could take a while and you look like you could use some rest."

My throat goes dry. "No, I'd like to wait for you to get back. To—I'd just like to wait, please."

I couldn't choke out the words. Didn't want Ford to give me that sympathetic look I always receive. He doesn't know me, doesn't know my past, but as soon I as I let slip what happened to me, the pity will start. The last thing I want is pity from a guy like him.

"Fine," he grunts. "You can wait here."

"You're too kind," I say to his retreating back.

When I'm alone, I drink some of the water and fight the urge to poke around his office just to spite him. What the hell is it with him giving me orders, anyway? It would show him if I did.

"Did you really see a dead body?" Comes a quiet voice

just as I'm contemplating going through Ford's drawers. A man like that has to have secrets.

I turn to the doorway and find a young girl leaning against the door jamb.

"I'm sorry?" My brain grinds to place her. Then I remember, she was there when Ford attacked that man in the Mustang.

"Mom said Uncle Ford had to go check out a dead body before she left." She ambles closer and I'm struck by the uncanny resemblance between them. "So, did you see it?"

"Isn't it past your bedtime?" I ask.

I'd been an only child and after...well, after, I hadn't really had much opportunity to socialize. To say I didn't know how to act around them, much less nosy pre-teens, is an understatement.

"I'm not six-years-old," she replies in a bored tone. "Besides, Mom isn't home and I didn't want to be alone. I'm Lexie, by the way."

"I'm Peyton." Knowing the feeling, I soften toward the girl. "I hope she wasn't dead, but I don't know. Sheriff Hadley and Ford went out to look."

"Are you and Uncle Ford like a couple or something?" she asks.

Baffled laughter erupts from my chest. "What? No!"

"You sure? He does that thing where he watches you

when he thinks you're not looking so I just figured you were."

He does? "He does?" I don't know whether to be creeped out or flattered. Erring on the side of caution, I go for unimpressed. "No, we're not dating. I'm just staying here for a couple of days." Considering I'm the only witness to a murder, maybe longer than I originally had planned.

"Mom didn't want to be around when the cops got here. She and Uncle Ford are like, allergic to them. Mom says it's 'cause Uncle Ford was interrogated after he went overseas." She lowers her voice to a whisper. "He killed someone and there was a big thing about it. Grandma and Grandpa thought he might go to prison."

A chill coats my skin and I wish I'd taken a shower before I'd changed clothes. The memory of being swallowed by cold, dark water from the lake seems to have frozen me right down to my very bones.

I don't want to jump to conclusions, but I'd been right when I thought there was something violent about Ford. Something dangerous. Something that screams at me to get the hell out of Dodge before shit gets even more real.

CHAPTER EIGHT
FORD

"So what do you know about this girl?" Hadley asks as the boat glides over the lake.

"You know as much as I do, Sheriff. She's a guest at the lodge. I haven't asked her life story."

Sheriff Hadley shines a high-powered flashlight over the surface of the water. "She seem like the reliable type to you?"

"Your guess is as good as mine. But I'll tell you this, I've seen the way people react to trauma. I don't think she was faking it, if that's what you're getting at."

Hadley grunts. "Let's take it all the way around to the far side of the lake and work our way around. With the dark, the distance, her estimation could have been off."

I point the boat toward the far side of the lake, my eyes scanning back and forth, straining against the lack of visibility. "Bear Lake is big, but it ain't huge. If something happened here like she says, it wouldn't be hard to find it."

"You'd be surprised."

"Is Windy Point hiding a hotbed of crime and intrigue I wasn't aware of?"

Mercy and I grew up in a town not far from here and moved to Windy Point when we were in elementary school when my father bought the lodge. It was the only place I felt at home when I left the Marines. The townspeople didn't exactly welcome me with open arms, but as long as I kept my head down and my nose clean, they didn't stick theirs too far into my business, which is how I prefer it.

Windy Point had been the quintessential small town as long as I've lived there. Local businesses trying to keep their heads above water. A thriving tourist season when the weather is right. Farm country and mountain country. Plenty of places to hide, to get lost in. A place where I didn't have to look over my shoulder.

"Not anymore than anywhere else, I reckon. We've got your domestic violence cases every once in a while. Sometimes a drunk and disorderly. Not as many murders, thank the Lord. The only big to-do was when you got home..."

He trails off, but neither of us needs him to finish the sentence for me to know what he was going to say.

Hadley clears his throat. "I didn't mean to imply..."

"Forget it," I bite out. "Let's just focus on finding this woman."

IT'S NEARLY MIDNIGHT BY THE TIME I HAUL MY TIRED ass back to the lodge, having said goodbye to Hadley a few minutes prior. Staying out on the water for hours without dinner in the freezing cold did little to improve my sunny disposition. I could only hope Peyton had changed her mind and decided to go back to her room to sleep. The last thing I want is to make small talk, but I know she has to be worried out of her mind. It only irritates me even more that I'm concerned about her.

I don't want to worry about her.

Don't want to think about her.

The sooner she leaves, the better.

The great room is empty, the embers in the fire have long since burned down. The night desk clerk nods at me as I walk by, but otherwise keeps her mouth shut. At least one of my employees has learned to follow directions. I make a mental note to fire Nell at least twice tomorrow for getting me involved in this mess.

Pushing through the door that leads to my small apartment and office space, I listen out for any sounds of movement. Hopefully Mercy and Lexie are asleep. I don't want to answer their questions or deal with their pestering, either. But the hall is dark and quiet. If they're awake, they're in my quarters.

The door to my office is cracked open and I see a sliver of Peyton asleep at my desk. Her blonde hair falls in a golden waterfall down her back. Her head rests on her folded arms and her pretty pink lips are parted slightly. She must have fought it for hours because there are dark circles underneath her eyes.

Because I want to watch her sleep, I nudge her shoulder until her eyes flicker open. "Peyton. Wake up, sunshine."

She stirs, moaning a little. "What?"

"C'mon, let's get you up to your room." I take her hand and help her to her feet while she's all docile and sweet.

"Ford?" she blinks until her eyes clear, then her hands fist on my shirt sleeves. "What happened? Did you find her?"

Oh, baby, what happened to you?

Instead of asking, I steer her toward the stairs. Her past is her business. I don't want to get more involved than I already am. "We didn't find her or any sign of her. Hadley is coming back tomorrow to search during the daylight with more officers."

Peyton visibly deflates and I have to brace myself when she stumbles. "What?" She shakes her head. "No, I definitely saw her. She was there. You have to find her."

It'd be easier if she was yelling at me. Instead, her voice

gets weaker. I want her to fight with me, to show me the spunky woman who I know is buried deep inside behind the fear, so I stop at the base of the stairs and give her a little shake. "Stop it." Her eyes widen at my barked order. "We don't know anything yet, other than what you saw. Hadley is a good man, a good cop. It's in his hands now. If there's any evidence of what happened, he'll find it."

Her chest inflates as she takes a deep breath. "No, you're right. I'm sorry."

"Don't apologize. Do you need help to your room?" I want her to say yes. I want to keep my hands on her, as messed up as that is. She may look like a spoiled brat, but there's a strength to her that I want to explore.

"No I think I've got it. Thanks," she pauses awkwardly. "For your help."

"I'll come and get you in the morning when Hadley gets here."

She stops a couple steps up, rubs at her eyes and yawning. "You don't have to do that."

"He'll want to speak to you again."

"Right. Well, thanks, but I'll meet you down here," she says.

"What?" My voice is rougher than I intend. I study her protective stance, her averted eyes. "You aren't afraid of me, are you?" When she doesn't answer, I nod, my lips twisting into a sardonic grin. I shouldn't be surprised, but I am. Did I think we had some sort of moment of understanding this afternoon? I couldn't have been more mistaken.

She tries to interject with what can only be an insincere apology, but I don't want to hear it. I lift a hand, cutting her off. "Save it. We're both tired. Get some sleep. Hadley will be here around 7."

I'd been an idiot for thinking our conversation had made her more comfortable.

"I'm just worn out," she offers, but I don't miss the way her arms tighten around her waist or how she glances upstairs toward the safety of her room.

Disgusted with myself that I'm disappointed, I shove my hands in my pockets. "Yeah," I reply, because I have no other polite words.

After an awkward silence, Peyton disappears upstairs like I'm gonna throw her back in the lake, and I head back to my office where I pour myself a generous shot of the whiskey I save for important occasions. Today hasn't been worth a celebration, but tomorrow is gonna be a shitshow. I could use the artificial buzz and distraction. Dawn will only bring more police, possibly the press, and God only knows how the guests will react to the possibility of a murder.

I'll have to ask Hadley how quiet we can keep this until it's confirmed. If he'll even speak to me without wondering whether or not I had anything to do with it.

Christ, how had everything gone so incredibly south?

So much for moving back to Windy Point for the peace and quiet.

I take my glass down the hall to my apartment. It's not much, certainly not as nice as the lodge itself, but it's an improvement of a cot in the desert. As I drink deeply, the whiskey settling into my stomach with a pleasant warmth, I study Mercy and Lexie. They must have fallen asleep trying to stay up to grill me about what had happened. They passed out in an incomprehensible tangle on the couch.

I'll have to talk to Mercy tomorrow, explain the situation and convince her to make other arrangements. They don't need to be around when everything goes down. Even if Peyton was somehow mistaken, news like this is guaranteed to reach the desk of an enterprising journalist. Once they delve into my background, everything I've been trying to bury will be fodder for the small town gossips all over again.

The last thing I need is for Mercy to get it into her head that her baby brother needs protecting. If anyone needs protecting, it's Mercy and Lexie. Especially if Peyton *was* right and there's a murderer in my backyard. If my bull headed sister won't see reason, I'll just call Mom and Dad and have them talk some sense into her. The sooner they leave the better.

I leave the two of them on the couch, sleeping peacefully for now. The secondary office space I keep setup in my room is lit by the desk lamp I can never remember to turn off. I polish off the rest of the whiskey and wish I'd brought the bottle along with me. Sleep seems near-impossible, but I know better than to get in the habit of self-medicating. I'd seen too many good men go the route of drowning themselves in booze and I was in no hurry to join them. I place the empty glass on the desk, sit, and start going through the guest records and security footage from the past couple hours.

An hour later, I have no more information than when I started, though I do have a headache brewing behind my eyes. All of our guests are accounted for, so no identification of the potential victim. The outdoor footage caught Peyton near dusk going to the water, but she disappeared into the trees. The angles were all wrong to get a clear view of the lake, so no tag or distinguishing features from the boat.

Resigned, I lean back in the chair as I attach my findings in an email, then send it to Hadley.

With the tedious work completed, I can't keep the thoughts of seeing Peyton facedown in the water from resurfacing. The whiskey does a wicked summersault in my stomach and I start to regret the indulgence. I scowl at my reflection in the bathroom mirror as I wait for the shower to heat up.

I should have insisted she see a doctor, but I'd been so

relieved she was conscious it didn't occur to me. Then I remind myself how she'd looked at me before she went to bed. She didn't want anything to do with me, that was certain. I can't say I blame her, considering the circumstances, but that doesn't explain why it pisses me the hell off. I should be glad she's keeping her distance. Hell, I even know she should, but that doesn't stop me from wanting her.

It doesn't matter.

Even if she wanted help from someone, she probably wouldn't want it from me.

CHAPTER NINE
PEYTON

THE GNAWING SENSATION of my stomach trying to cannibalize itself wakes me and the moment I open my eyes I realize it's not because I'm hungry.

I'm as far from hungry as it's possible to be. In fact, the mere thought of food makes me want to sprint to the bathroom and vomit. A cold, sour sweat coats my skin, leaving me clammy and sticky despite the shower I'd taken the night before.

Because I want to curl under the blankets and pretend like nothing's changed, I force myself out of bed and pad across the room to throw open the curtains. My hands grip the frame until the urge to fling them closed subsides. In the distance, I can see police vehicles and eve farther out, boats on the water slowly gliding back and forth across its surface.

So it wasn't a dream.

No, it's just a waking nightmare.

As soon as I finish talking to the sheriff again to see if he found anything, I'm going to cancel the rest of my reservation and get the heck out of dodge. I have no intention of repeating past mistakes and can find another paradise to paint. Moving on would be the best for everyone involved. The decision makes my stomach settle and I dress quickly, wanting to get it all over with so I can move on.

My cell rings before I can leave the room. Uncle Brad again.

Knowing if I ignore his call it will only cause him to be more relentless, I answer. "Hello?"

"Peyton," he responds and by the grave tone in his voice, I can tell that whatever reason he's calling for can't be a good one.

"Uncle Brad? Is everything okay?"

His sigh fills my ears. "Unfortunately, no, sweetheart. I have some bad news and I think the best way to handle it is to just tell you right out."

I sit on the edge of the bed. "What is it?"

"The money in your trust...it's gone."

The tension goes out of my body and my insides turn to liquid. "Gone? How could it be gone?"

My brain buzzes and I have to ask him to repeat his answer. Even then, I only catch a few words: lawyer, stole, embezzle, police. I don't know how I manage to have a coherent conversation with him because the buzzing in my head is so loud, I can hardly think.

"Uncle Brad?" I interrupt when I can't listen any longer. "I have to go. No, I'm sorry," I say before he can convince me to keep talking. "I'll call you later and we'll talk more about it."

I feel bad for hanging up on him mid-sentence, but any more and I would have screamed. No more money in the trust. The trust that had paid for my therapy, the mortgage and upkeep on my parents' house. The trust I'd been depending on for my little wild adventure. Gone.

Defeated, I decide to skip doing my makeup. Who cares what I look like? I certainly don't. I just want to get this over with.

The downstairs is full of people with their faces pressed against the glass window, watching the spectacle on the other side. The low murmur of their voices echoes up to the second floor. My stomach turns as I descend the stairs and I pass a hand over my hair out of habit, wondering if they're already gossiping about me. Certainly they couldn't have found out about my past so quickly.

My presence goes relatively unnoticed until I step into the front desk's line of sight, where Nell spots me and comes out proffering a steaming mug of coffee. "I made it the way you like," she says with a motherly smile that goes straight to my tender heart.

I accept the mug and try to look around for Ford without being obvious. "Thank you, that's very sweet. Um, do you know where I can find the sheriff?"

She goes back behind the counter and adjusts her glasses with a mournful sound. "He should be back any minute. Why don't you wait in Ford's office for them?"

The thought of being surrounded by his things, in his space, makes me take a step backward. I want to keep as much distance between us as possible. Call it paranoia, call it self-preservation. It doesn't matter. Ford is an enigma I have no interest in solving.

"That's okay," I tell Nell, "I think I'll just wait out here. Do they have any updates?" I can't help but ask.

Nell leans over the counter, propping her chin on her hand. "Ford asked Hadley to keep things quiet for the time being." Her Southern accent clips the end of the word *being* into *been*.

"I'm sure he did," I mutter under my breath, thinking of the conversation I had with his niece. Who had he been accused of killing and how had he gotten away with it? Nell and the others seem to like him, but there are charismatic people who hide their evil alter-egos all the time. I know that all too well.

Except Ford is as opposite from charismatic as it's possible to be. You'd think if he were guilty he'd try a little more to clear suspicion rather than attract it by being so confrontational. I recall the argument with the woman a few days ago. No, Ford certainly doesn't have a problem with getting on someone's bad side.

"What's that, dear?" Nell asks.

"Nothing," I reply, then nod to one of the empty tables on the deck. "I think I'll take one of those muffins from the bar and wait outside."

She's interrupted by the ringing of the landline and gives me a smile and a wave.

"I heard a kid drowned last night..."

"They found her body washed up on shore..."

"That scary owner guy killed a man because he was sleeping with his woman..."

If the situation weren't so dire, the misinformed whispers from the crowd might have made me chuckle. At least no one knew I was involved...yet. And they won't, so long as I have it my way.

The blueberry muffin I snag from the breakfast bar smells amazing and even though my stomach revolts at the thought of food, I force down a few large bites along with several gulps of coffee. My hands ache for a pencil and pad of paper to sketch the scene in front of me. One of the things I learned in therapy was to draw to keep my mind from racing. Maybe it leeched a bit of the natural joy I got from art for a time, but it helped to distract me.

I could use the distraction now.

I sense Ford before I see him. The muscles in my neck and shoulders clench and the hairs on my arm prickle. My hands clench on the nearly empty coffee cup. I'm self-aware enough to realize my reaction to him can't merely be fear. If that was the case, I'd still be in my room. I wouldn't be out here, watching, waiting for him...and that's what truly scares me. Not that he's big and rough, that his direct gaze makes my insides shiver. Not his past, whatever it is.

What scares me the most...is not being scared of him at all.

CHAPTER TEN
FORD

Lack of sleep and a headache from straining to see through the murky water put me in a foul mood. Not that I'm normally in a perky one.

"How much longer do you think you'll keep at it?" I ask Hadley as we disembark from his boat and trek back up to the lodge.

Hadley looks about as good as I feel. He rubs at the dark smudges beneath his eyes. Guess I wasn't the only one who got little to no rest the night before. "Couple more hours, but we could only spare a couple guys and they're just volunteering. Can't waste anymore manpower if we're coming up with squat."

"Sooner the better. All this nonsense is gonna start scaring off business." I'd already had a cancelation from a current customer who didn't want to come back next month for their spring break vacation.

Hadley pauses and narrows his eyes at me. "Nonsense, huh? I thought you believed her."

I shrug, my gaze lifting from the trail to find Peyton. It doesn't take long. That woman always seems to be right in the middle of chaos. How she manages to derail everything in such a short amount of time, I'll never know.

"It's not that I don't believe her. Shit, Paul. Just want this over with."

He sighs and we continue on. "You and me both."

Not to mention the longer this drags out, the more I'll have to worry about Mercy, who took my request to leave about as well as I anticipated. Stubbornness must be a family trait.

In a compromise, I threw money at the both of them to go shopping or whatever a couple towns over with strict instructions to keep themselves busy until Hadley and the other cops cleared out. Both in case they did find a body, or on the off chance reporters showed up.

So far I've been lucky on both counts.

Hadley pauses at the top of the steps, nodding to the older couple who own the town bakery and often stay at the lodge for a little getaway. The wife, Mrs. Margaret, was also the biggest mouth this side of the Mississippi so if I have any doubts about word getting around they were squashed.

Peyton gets to her feet as Hadley reaches her side. Her face is carefully blank and clean of makeup, leaving her looking even more innocent and vulnerable than usual.

I keep a couple steps behind Hadley and prop myself on an elbow. Technically, he shouldn't need me involved, but I can't seem to make myself go back inside. I don't want to give a damn, but I also don't want to leave her alone. Not when it looks like a stiff wind could knock her over.

Peyton gives me a look over Hadley's shoulder like she's wondering what I'm doing here and I glower back at her.

Nell, who must have been watching the security cameras from the front desk, comes out with a tray of steaming hot coffee and several mugs. She tops off Peyton's, then hands Hadley and I the remaining mugs.

"Here you are Sheriff," she says.

"Thank you, Nell, I appreciate it."

"You have a message for you when you're finished here, boss," Nell tells me with a pointed look.

"Appreciate it. I'll be back in a few," I tell her. "Leave it on my desk."

"Y'all need anything else while I'm here?"

"No, thank you," Hadley and Peyton chime in.

"We're good," I say.

With one last curious glance backward, Nell goes back inside. I push the curiosity of a message to the back of my mind.

"Good morning, Ms. Rhodes," Hadley says.

"Sheriff," she says a little breathlessly. If possible, her face has lost even more color, leaving only a slash of pink at her cheeks from the cold. Damn woman is gonna faint again if she doesn't take better care of herself. Knowing she'd only bite my head off, I take a deep swallow of coffee and am pleased when she does the same.

I frown and look away.

No reason why I should be staring at her unless I want another rude awakening.

"We've searched the whole area," Hadley begins. "Are you absolutely sure about what you saw? Where?"

Peyton crosses her arms above her chest and her lips pinch together for a second. "Yes, just as I told you. Do you want me to r-ride out with you to prove it?" Despite the tremor in her voice, she shakes back her hair defiantly. At least she's a brave little bird, shaky, but brave. I'd bet anything going out on that water is the last thing she wants to do.

I don't have to check Hadley to know he's probably thinking the same thing. He may be a local, small-town cop, but he's not stupid.

"No, ma'am, we've got it covered. We're gonna wrap it up shortly, though, if we don't find anything. No use worrying everyone if there's nothing else to go on." Hadley pauses and lays a comforting hand on her arm. "Is there someone we can call for you. Husband, boyfriend. Your family? You seem pretty shaken up. There's a counselor in town, but—"

"Thanks," she interrupts, "but no. I'll be fine. I appreciate you letting me know. I'm sorry for the trouble I've caused."

Hadley adjusts his hat. "It's no trouble. We've got your contact information if we do find anything."

She nods. "Yes, please give me a call if you do."

Hadley turns to me. "We'll be out of your hair soon, Ford. Sherry and I will be by sometime this week for date night—if she doesn't kill me before then."

"We'll have a table for you," I reply, my eyes still on Peyton, whose turned to look out toward the water where the other volunteers have started to pack up.

"Thank you for your help, Ms. Rhodes," Hadley says before he excuses himself to go and help. "We'll be in touch if we need anything."

Peyton visibly deflates as Hadley disappears into the distance.

"No evidence is a good thing," I say, but she shakes her head and says, "I'd rather know for sure. Otherwise it's a huge question mark in my head. It'll drive me crazy."

She places her mug carefully on the deck railing and turns to face me directly for the first time. Before she can apologize, again, I lift a hand and wave away her empty words. I've heard it all before. "Don't worry about it. I've got work to do."

"Ford, I'm serious," she starts.

"So am I. No need to apologize. You'll let Nell know if you need anything? Checkout is Friday, right? It's been a memorable stay, but I'm sure you'll be excited to put this place in your rearview."

She makes a pained face. "You believe me, don't you?" She asks after a pause. "I'm not sure Hadley does, at least not completely."

"He wouldn't have spent all morning out there if he didn't. It doesn't matter what I think."

"Yes—" she starts to shout, then glances around as heads turn in our direction. "Yes, it does. It matters to me. He would be more convinced if they'd found something, anything, but he only has my word to go on. The word of a stranger."

"Hadley is a good guy. He's just doing his job. Besides, I was there. I believe you."

Her eyes grow wet and an uncomfortable knot takes up residence in my chest. I shift from foot to foot. "Are you okay?" I ask.

She clears her throat and shakes her head. "I'm fine. But you don't have to say that to make me feel better."

"Do I seem like the kind of person who caters to anyone's feelings?"

Peyton gave me a small smile. "Definitely not."

"Listen, it's been a rough couple days. Why don't you help yourself to the bar, on me, and relax. As for what happened last night, let's just forget about it, okay? No hard feelings."

"Are you sure? I didn't mean to make it weird." She sighs. "I, just, I've been through a lot and this is pushing all of my buttons. It's honestly a miracle I haven't lost my shit by now. I mean, like an epic breakdown. I don't know if it's better that they haven't found anything or worse. I think it's the not knowing that's even worse." Her panicked voice is sharp and getting louder the more she goes on. She gestures wildly.

This time, I do step forward. I place my hands on her arms. "Hey, everything will be fine. You're going to go get lunch, get a drink, and let me handle Hadley. I've got you."

At my words, Peyton stills, the breath catching in her chest. "What did you say?"

My lips twitch. "I said everything will be fine." I push her back in the direction of the french doors. "Now go. Take care of yourself before you pass out again and I have to carry you." Or before I do something stupid and kiss her until we both forget what's happening.

A laugh bursts from her lips and dances briefly in her eyes, then she turns and reaches out a hand for the door-knob. "Why don't you join me?" she blurts out.

"Join you?"

"Dinner, later. My treat. To thank you for everything. And to apologize for the way I acted last night after everything you've done for me. For saving me. Believing me. I owe you."

"You don't owe me anything."

She rolls her eyes. "Do you want food or not?"

God, but I don't want to tell her no. I knew the second I saw her standing at the desk with all that hair and her perky smile that I wanted nothing to do with her. That she was trouble. The worst kind of trouble.

"Make it drinks," I tell her, "and we have a deal."

THE LAST OF THE VOLUNTEERS ARE GONE AFTER CHECK-out at one and I can finally have some peace and quiet. Or I would if the gaggle of women at my back could stop their hen pecking.

"So I did some digging," Mercy began the second I was finished with the last customer.

I spin around in the stool and raise a brow. "Did you? About what?"

Mercy scoffs and Nell takes a step out of my office where she'd been copying papers. "About the girl." She wiggles her brows. "The one you've been staring at like she's a steak and you're a starving dog."

Mercy's bawdy laugh fills the space. "He is a dog!"

"Why are you here again?" I ask her. "Don't you have someone else you can bother?"

"Lexie is out with some friends she met in town and Frank is at the shop with his car."

"Frank the Mustang guy?"

"Hell, no, I ditched his ass. I met Frank at the bar."

A sterling character reference. "Get to the point, Merce, I've got things to do."

"So, anyway, I did some digging on this Peyton girl."

That gets my attention. "You what?"

Mercy plops in the seat next to me and spins to lean toward Nell. "I mean, who wouldn't, right? This girl shows up and shit starts to go down. That can't be a coincidence."

"You had no business doing that," I say to her.

"Please. It was absolutely my business. Especially when you go around making eyes at her."

"C'mon, Mercy, we're not fourteen years old anymore. I'm not making eyes at anyone."

"Pfft! Oh, please. You may have disappeared over the past five years, but I've been your sister for your whole life. I was there when you made eyes at Marjorie Lennox. I was there when you made eyes at Julie Smith. I know you. And you may be some badass Marine, but I'm still your big sister and it's still my job to protect you however I can."

"You don't need to protect me."

"Someone has to. Anyway." Mercy turns to Nell and gestures with a hand. "You wouldn't *believe* what I found out about our little Peyton."

"I'm not listening to this," I announce and turn back to the computer in front of me.

"You don't have a choice," Mercy says.

"For God's sake," Nell mutter-screams. "What did you find out?"

I give a brief thought to leaving. If Peyton wanted everyone to know her history, she'd tell it herself. Like me, if I were interested in playing armchair psychologist, I'd talk about what happened to me.

That sure as hell doesn't stop me from listening to what Mercy has to say next.

"Well, I did some searching and she's still using her legal name so she must not be trying to hide it. Anyway, some tweakers broke into her parents house and robbed the place. They took the family hostage and then killed her parents."

"That's awful," Nell says.

Mercy leans forward, her eyebrows raised. "That's not the end. Peyton was in the house when all this went down. The tweakers tied her up in the basement. Held her parents for hours while she listened to them torture them. When they were done, hours later, they shot her and left her for dead."

Nell dabs at her eyes with a tissue. "Sweet Jesus. That poor baby."

"It was all over the internet. There are dozens of articles and interviews. Apparently, she was in a psych ward for a while. Then, like, became one of those people who didn't leave their house, like ever."

"Mercy," I say.

"Anyway, from what I understand, it wouldn't be out of the realm of possibility for her to be imagining the whole thing. Making it up. Having a break from reality."

"Mercy," I say more firmly.

She gives me a look. "I'm just *saying* Ford. Think past your dick and take a step back. We don't know this woman. You only know what she's telling you and—"

I get to my feet and when I speak, my voice is calm, quiet. I know from facing down some of the most evil people on this earth it's not yelling that gets someone's attention, it's the absolute certainty in a hushed delivery. "What matters here is that I believe her, Mercy. This isn't any of your business."

"But—"

"No buts. I believe her and I don't want to hear you saying this to anyone else. She deserves her privacy. Is that clear?" They don't answer and I move toward my office. "For the record, I was in her position not too long ago and no one believed me. Until we know otherwise, you'd be wise to give her the benefit of the doubt. You don't know what's true unless you were there. Were you with me overseas when I watched two of my best friends get blown to pieces?" When they don't answer, I nod. "I didn't think so. Don't judge her unless you've been in her shoes."

"Ford, I—" Mercy begins.

"Save it. And you know what, Mercy? If you're going to be here, you need to help out. No more freeloading. And don't either of you say a word about this to anyone else or to Peyton. Unless you want to find somewhere else to stay."

Mercy sputters. "What about Lexie?"

"Lexie can stay. God knows it'd be less of a circus here than following you all over the country with your boy toys. Now if you two don't mind, I've got work to do."

My head pounds as I stride back to my office. Having that drink can't happen soon enough.

CHAPTER ELEVEN

PEYTON

I SHOULD HAVE LISTENED to Ford and stayed at the lodge and rested, but I didn't.

Waiting around while everyone else cleared out would have only driven me crazy and I needed to keep moving or it would give me too much time to think. I wanted to be surrounded by people, activity, sounds.

Life.

So I found myself in the center of town again, although this time, I didn't have my parents' trust to blow money on, so I window shop and wonder if having drinks with Ford is just one more in a long line of mistakes.

The colorful sign for Splatters Studio catches my eye as I walk down the sidewalk and I remember Alice's job offer. I hadn't really given it serious thought at the time as I'd just been planning to pass through, but now...everything is different. I don't have the money to fall back on and with the murder I don't feel like I can leave.

I hesitate on the crosswalk at an intersection as I ponder whether to go in or to head back to my car. If I stay, it means facing what happened that night, something I've barely been able to do with my own past, let alone involving myself in someone else's trauma. It means facing Ford, and whatever is—or isn't—there. It means staying when every instinct inside me is screaming at me to run. To hide, like I did for so long after I lost my parents.

The safety net I've had for so long is gone. This wild adventure I'd begun is over before it really began, but this time I don't want to be the girl who locked herself away because she was too scared. I want to be the kind of girl who can face her fears and come out on the other side stronger. As much as I want to be her, at the center of it, I don't know if I am and I'm terrified to let myself down.

I don't know why, but in that moment of indecision, I hear Ford's voice from our conversation earlier.

"I've got you," he'd said. Effortlessly. Like he believed it.

Maybe for a second, I did too.

My feet move in the direction of Splatters before I give myself the chance to think about what I'm doing. There's a birthday party going on, but the owner Alice spots me the second the bell jingles when I open the door.

She crosses to my side with a smile on her face. "You

haven't left yet?" she asks and pulls me in for a hug. "I wasn't sure I'd see you again."

"Actually, I was wondering if the offer for a job was still open. If it is, I'd like to take it." Butterflies flutter in my stomach and I feel faint, but not because I'm scared this time. Because I'm excited. I shouldn't be on the cusp of all the terrible things that have happened, but I'll take my positive moments where I can get them. "I'm going to be in the area longer than I expected."

Alice's head tips to the side as she considers me. "I have to say I'm surprised. Pleased, but surprised. Why don't you follow me back to the office and we'll get the employment paperwork out of the way?" She takes me by the arm and leads me to a small, but stylish office in the back of the building. "What made you change your mind?" she asks as she takes a seat behind her desk and begins rifling through drawers.

I sit opposite her and place my purse in my lap. Shrugging, I say, "Unfinished business."

She passes me a manilla folder and a pen. "Why don't you get started on these while we get to know each other. What got you interested in art?"

Considering my words carefully, I open the folder and begin filling out the paperwork. "Originally, I was very interested in portraits. The people behind the mask. Capturing the emotions behind the expression, that sort of thing. Pulling the true person out from behind the veneer."

"You'll have to show me some of your work sometime."

I shrug, keeping my eyes on the forms and applying myself to keeping the pen steady as I write. "I don't really do portrait work anymore. Not in," my voice breaks and I clear my throat. "Not in a couple years now. I work primarily with landscapes these days, " I finish.

At the middle of it all, I approach my art with quiet meticulousness that characterized my childhood. My mom used to tell me my art was the only place where I truly let myself go, where I connected with people. I haven't been able to connect much these days. My therapist likes to say I paint landscapes now because I'm afraid to look too deep into another person. Well, whether he was right or not we'll never know because I haven't painted a portrait since the day before my parents died.

"One of your landscapes, then," Alice comments.

I glance up, lost in thought. Then I catch the thread of the conversation again. "Right, of course. I'll have to remember to bring a piece sometime."

The portraits I used to do sit forgotten in Uncle Brad's attic. I used to think I could find the answers I was looking for when I did someone's portrait.

I used to think I knew everything.

But the truth is, no matter how hard you try, sometimes there are parts of life that just don't have any answers.

"That sounds lovely. Now are you staying at the lodge or have you found someplace in town?"

"I have a couple more days I've already paid for, but after that I actually have no idea," I admit. I finish the stack of papers, close them in the folder, then hand them over. "To be honest, I hadn't planned to stay, but circumstances have changed so I'm sort of winging it."

"The great thing about small towns, if there is such a thing, is that we all are in each other's business." She grins and gestures for me to get up. "I've got some friends around town who might have a place where you can stay. I've got a small house, but it may not be to your taste."

Touched, I scoop up my purse and follow her back to the main room eagerly. Finally something is going my way. "I'm not picky, really. I'm grateful."

"That's a start," she says.

"I appreciate your help. I'd love to know more about what we'll be doing here."

"Of course. Let me give you an overview and then, if you're still interested, we'll go take a look at the house."

Before I can thank her again, she's off. Alice leads me to each of the smaller rooms. "These are primarily for small get togethers. Sometimes we have birthday parties, dates, classes, business events, and so forth. You'll be responsible for coordinating with the person arranging each event, the supplies, making sure they have everything they need. If you're up to it, I'd also love to have you teach a class or two, maybe run a Paint and Wine night."

The thought causes those butterflies to triple. "I'd love to teach. Anything you need me to do, really."

It isn't just because I need the money and want to stay close to the town, although both of those are important factors. Working here will require that I get out of my room, interact with other people. I'll get to know the locals and keep my skills fresh at the same time. Maybe by getting to know them, it'll help me discover what happened on the lake. It may not, but I feel like I owe it to the woman to at least try.

HOURS LATER, I RETURN BACK TO THE LODGE WITH A job, and a place to stay once my stay is up. The house Alice owns isn't really anything to write home about. If Uncle Brad were to see it, he'd think I was joking. Located on the far side of Bear Lake, it's a small, one bedroom, shotgun style construction built sometime in the tail end of the 1940s. The walls are wood paneled. The floors are chipped, cheap linoleum. The bathroom is covered in an obnoxious pink tile that reminds me of Pepto Bismol.

But it's got a roof, sturdy locks, and Alice is letting me rent it for ridiculously cheap.

Maybe there's something to this small-town thing.

Nell and Ford's sister give me the same assessing look from behind the front counter when I burst through the doors, but I'm floating too high to read too much into it. I take the steps back to my room two at a time and when I open the door to find it dark again, it doesn't even phase me. Tomorrow is my last full day at the lodge, so I take a few minutes while I'm feeling energized to pack. Somehow my belongings had exploded all over the place.

That done, I change into a pair of skinny jeans, a fitted flannel shirt, and run a brush through my hair. I don't exactly consider dinner and drinks with Ford a date, so I don't do more than swipe on some mascara. As I'm walking out of the room, I check my phone and find a missed call from Uncle Brad, which I resolve to return...later.

I lock eyes with Ford the second I step out of my room. The grand open first floor makes it easy for him to watch as I come down the stairs and cross the lobby. Nell and his sister had disappeared. The lobby is empty save for us.

My mouth goes dry at being the center of his focus. Suddenly shy, I tuck my hair behind my ear and focus my gaze on his chin. "Hey," I say, when I reach the counter. I can feel his eyes studying me and I flush.

Ford comes out from behind the counter and I nearly

swallow my own tongue. He's wearing his shitkicker boots, jeans that hug powerful thighs and cup him in all the right places, and a tight, long-sleeved henley that I want to peel off.

"I've got steaks and veggies from the grill for tonight, whiskey and wine. Sound good?"

"Sounds perfect. Where exactly are we going?" I ask as he retrieves a fabric bag with clicking bottles and a tray full of food from behind the counter. "Here, let me take that," I offer and shoulder the bag.

"Thanks. One of our rooms is going through renovations. It's a mess, but it has the best view of Bear Lake and the mountains. If you were here for landscapes, it's where you want to be."

"It sounds amazing. I appreciate you going to the trouble."

He glances over his shoulder. "It's no trouble, Peyton."

Inspiration strikes and I say, "So this room, it's covered in like plastic sheets and everything, right?"

"Yeah, probably."

"Wait here just a second," I tell him and run to my room. I come out a few minutes later with a bag full of supplies my easel, and two large canvases. I'm loaded down with stuff, but I don't care. One night of fun is worth it.

"What are you doing?" he asks warily and the look on his face is so comical, I laugh.

"Relax, we're just going to have some fun. I'm not the only one who needs to let go a little."

"I don't need to let go of anything."

I snort as I follow him up to the third level of the lodge I didn't even know was there. "Your wound up tighter than I am. It's probably why you can be such a jerk."

He eyes me as he holds the door to the room open. "I'll remember that next time I decide to feed you."

"Wow," I say as I walk in the room. "You weren't kidding. This place just keeps getting more and more beautiful." The windows mimic the first floor lobby, floor to ceiling and on the other side is a breathtaking view of Bear Lake. "I'd kill for a place like this."

"My parents used to live up here before we converted the back rooms downstairs to an apartment. My sisters and I grew up here. I've been updating it the past couple months as I can."

I turn to him. "You're a handyman, too?"

"When I have the free time," he says with a shrug. "C'mon, I'm starving and you look like you could use a drink."

He pulls two sawhorses together, covers them with a piece of extra plywood and drapes a clean drop cloth over the top. I pull two folding chairs over and give them a quick wipe-down after setting my supplies down by the door.

Ford plates up the food and pours himself some whiskey and me a full glass of wine.

"This smells amazing," I tell him as I take my seat.

"You'll have to thank Nell, she's the one who makes sure I get fed at night."

"I'll do that. She didn't look too happy to see me this afternoon when I got back." He flicks on a lamp and then comes to sit opposite me at our makeshift table. "I hope I didn't do anything wrong."

Ford digs into his steak, chews. "Nothing like that, but I have to be honest, my sister did some digging about you."

I sit back in my chair, my smile evaporating. I inhale half my wine for something to do. "She did?"

"She's a little protective, but that doesn't excuse her behavior. Trust me, I've already reamed her for invading your privacy like that."

The wine makes me head feel a little fuzzy. "Don't be upset with her. I'm sure it's only natural to want to find out more about a stranger. Especially considering the circumstances."

Ford reaches across the table and covers my free hand with his own. "I'm sorry that happened to you, Peyton. I'll make sure Mercy doesn't spread it around."

The genuine understanding in his expression makes me want to melt. "Thank you. Don't worry about it. The news is sure to spread at some point."

He takes a sip of his whiskey and the second he removes his hand I want to ask him to put it back. I guess my art wasn't the only thing I've been missing. Companionship, closeness. The simple act of being touched by another person. All I can think about is all the other places I want his hands.

"Do you want to talk about it?" he asks softly.

"For once, I'd like to talk about anything but that," I try not to put a pleading tone in my voice, but I can't help it.

"Your wish," he says and nods at my food. "Now eat, then you can show me why you dragged all that shit up here."

I pause as I taste perfectly seasoned red potatoes. "You don't think I'm crazy?"

He smirks. "Baby, I've only known you a couple days and I'd love to put you in a straight jacket sometimes, but I don't think you're crazy."

CHAPTER TWELVE
FORD

"I FEEL LIKE AN IDIOT," I say as I stand still for her to wrap an apron around my waist. "I'm not a 1950's housewife."

Peyton snorts. "You'll thank me when you don't have paint splotches all over your pretty clothes."

I glance down at the henley and jeans I'm wearing. "You're delusional if you think these clothes are pretty."

Her eyes linger long enough on my body that the alcohol in my bloodstream ignites. I give half a thought to telling her if she's worried about getting paint on my clothes that she can take them off, but I think better of it and gulp down the rest of my drink instead. More alcohol sounds like a better plan.

"Just shut up and wear the damn apron, Collier."

"Yes, ma'am."

She refills my glass of whiskey and her own with more

wine, then goes about setting out paints and setting up two canvases, distributing brushes and god knows what else. I pull up two stools just to watch her. Mercy hadn't been totally wrong when she said I watched Peyton. Before it'd been with a wariness, like an animal observing a new, fascinating creature. Now I don't have to look away. Honestly, I don't give a fuck. It could be the whiskey, could be the way she looks at me over her shoulder, her blonde hair all wild and her eyes bright with laughter.

Now that the heavy conversation has passed and we're both thoroughly plied with booze, there's a lightness about her I haven't had the pleasure of seeing before. She giggles as she stumbles back from the bathroom, having retrieved two mugs of water.

"Nice," I say and sip my whiskey.

"Shut up or this will turn into a nude lesson."

I lift a brow and gesture with my glass. "This just got more interesting. Feel free to strip anytime, sunshine."

Drunk Peyton smiles and I find myself smiling back. She skip-stumbles over to my side and takes my glass from my hand, shushing me when I argue. "You can have it back in a few minutes. You promised you'd come paint with me. I've heard Marines are quick learners, I'm sure you can keep up." She tugs me by the hand and leads me to the easel. My body follows her without protest, like we're magnets and I can't help but go where she leads.

Scowling at the canvas, I take the proffered paintbrush. "I don't know what the fuck I'm doin' here."

"The first rule of art is there are no rules," she says, sipping her wine, her head tilted as she studies me. "This is just for fun. I haven't had fun with my work in so long. I miss it. Just play with me for a while Ford. You don't always have to be so serious. It'll be good for you to let loose. I think you need it."

I slop the paint brush in a random pot of red. "I can think of other ways I'd rather let loose and play with you," I say. Peyton chokes on her wine and I send her a grin, pointing my paint brush at her. "Careful there, young lady."

"Focus, Ford," but she's laughing so hard she can barely get the words out. "This is supposed to be your masterpiece."

"Right," I say and turn back to the canvas. I slop some of the red on it's surface and angle my head. "My masterpiece."

Peyton dips her own brush in a pot of blue and drags it across the canvas much more artfully. She takes another sip of wine and adds more blue, then a hint of black. When she glances over and jerks her head to my own, I turn back and squint at the dripping mass of red. Sighing, I choose colors at random, not even really thinking about the process. The scent of paint and Peyton's perfume surrounds me until they intertwine. I won't ever be able to smell paint without thinking of her. Like the fumes, she's soaking into my skin. Like the paint on my fingertips, she staining a part of me and no amount of scrubbing will ever get her out.

My "art" is little more than a kindergartener's efforts, but when I take a step back, I recognize the setting of the night we lost Tate. The night that's so burned into my brain I'd recreated it without thinking. The blue-black shadows of the dunes. The deep maroon splashes of blood. The whites of his eyes. The sprinkle of stars in the infinite night.

I turn my back on it and find Peyton studying her own creation intently. Downing the rest of my whiskey, I dump the brushes in the cleaning solution and move behind her as she works. Her body moves against mine and I don't even think she notices until she leans against me, her back to my front and sighs a little.

My hands go to her hips, pressing her more firmly against me, as I study what looks like a freeform landscape. It's the lake. That night. The boat, the dock, the water. What had started as a fun little experiment had turned up two terrible moments, for both of us.

Wanting, needing, to take that terrible moment away for her, I turn her around in my arms and study her face. Her lips tremble as she looks up at me. I reach past her, dip my fingers in paint, then keep my eyes on hers as I finger-paint a line over her collarbone.

She inhales sharply, then shivers from the coolness of

the slick paint against her skin. Eyes bright, but not from the wine this time, she shifts and her hands go to my waistband. Without words, she slides her hands up my abdomen, taking the hem of the henley along with it. It goes up and over my head, then flutters to the ground somewhere behind me. Peyton dips her fingers in paint, then traces a line down the center of my chest to the top of my jeans.

"This is the best paint by numbers ever," she says throatily.

I tug on her shirt, paint smudging the material. "Take this off," I order.

The corner of her lips tilt up. She begins to unbutton it, slowly, torturously, then peels it off, leaving her in a skin-tight pair of jeans, feet bare, with only the thin material of her bra. I sweep her hair over her shoulder leaving streaks of paint in my wake and kiss the sweet curve of her neck. Her arms twine around my shoulders and I can feel the sticky tips of her fingers on my skin.

I cup her jaw with both hands and take her mouth, needy, greedily, and she meets my efforts with matching enthusiasm. We crash into the wall next to the canvases and she tries to crawl up my body.

"You feel so good," she says breathlessly as I nibble at her throat.

Her gasp brings me back to reality. I grasp her arms and

push her back, trying to give myself some breathing room. "Wait."

She peers up at me, her lips beautifully red, her cheeks flushed and her eyes trusting and sweet. "What's wrong?"

"You're drunk. I should get you back to your room, let you get some sleep."

Peyton blinks once. Twice. "What?"

"I don't want to take advantage of you. You've been through a lot the past couple days."

Her hands come to my chest and she pushes until we switch positions. "If anyone is taking advantage, it's gonna be me taking you. I'm not fragile, Ford. You aren't going to break me."

Paint-smeared fingers glide down my biceps, then grip my hands and pin them to the wall. "Keep these here," she says.

I should stop her, every rational voice in my head is screaming to stop her, but when she undoes the apron at my waist, then goes for my belt buckle, my mouth goes dry and I forget how to speak.

She tugs my jeans down as she gets to her knees. I'm not fully hard, but it doesn't stop her from taking me in her hand. "Fuck," I gasp as her free hand fondles the heavy weight of my testicles and strokes my cock with the other.

Remnants of paint streak across my skin, but I couldn't care less. Her eyes flick up to me and I have to wonder if she's using me like a new medium, the artist and the subject. Needing to do something with my hands, sift them through her hair, tugging on the strands and making her gasp in the back of her throat.

When she strokes me until precum glistens at the tip, I take my cock in hand, covering hers, and say, "Suck me."

Her eyes brighten at the order and she looks at me under her lashes as she scoots forward, suddenly obedient. Lips parted, she holds utterly still as I paint her lips with precum. Her tongue darts out to lick away the liquid, the tip of her tongue flicking against the flushed head of my dick.

My fingers tighten in her hair. "Tease," I admonish and her lips curve in a smile just before she wraps them around me, sucking hard.

I throw my head back against the wall. "Fuck, Peyton." On a keening whine, she sucks me deep, her tongue lashing against me and her lips forming a tight seal. Unable to control myself, my hips thrust forward and her eyes widen in surprise at the invasion before her throat relaxes and she takes me as deep as she can, her eyes locked on mine until I screw mine shut. Feeling her and seeing her is too much. It's been so long and I want to make it last.

Her hands work in perfect rhythm with her mouth, gliding and tugging until my legs go numb from pleasure.

On a growl, I take my dick in one hand and bring her to her feet with the other. "Strip," I tell her as I kick off my boots and tug my pants and underwear the rest of the way off, leaving me naked, my cock jutting out in front of me, her eyes glued to it as I stroke in anticipation.

She glances around then, spotting the bed covered in another drop cloth, tugs me toward it and I follow, hesitations forgotten. Pausing to turn, she reaches back and undoes the catch to her bra and bares her breasts. Unable to restrain myself, I push her back on the bed, ignoring her yelp of surprise and catch us both with a hand on the mattress to control our fall.

As I busy myself tasting and nibbling on her nipples, she fidgets beneath me, alternating between clutching at my head and trying to work her jeans and panties down her legs.

"Help me," she demands when it proves to be too much. Her hands go back to my head and she pulls me close. "Don't stop."

I chuckle against her skin. "Well, which is it?"

"Ford, please," she moans.

With one hand, I plump one breast to my lips and lick at my leisure and with the other, I still her bucking hips long enough to work her jeans down and off one leg. The remains dangle from the other because she locks her thighs around me like she doesn't ever want me to leave. My cock pressed against the wetness between her legs convinces me there's no other place I'd rather be.

She tugs me back up to her mouth as she makes greedy little noises in the back of her throat. I want to take my time, to get my mouth on her and make her come at least once before I take her, but she doesn't give me the chance. Her hand steals down between us, then locks around my dick, bringing it to her opening.

I break the kiss and exhale violently as her legs tighten and the head slips just enough inside that my vision goes white. "Fuck, wait a second."

"I want you inside me," she says against my ear. "Please, Ford, I want to feel you."

My hips move involuntarily as I slip a little bit deeper with each thrust. "You feel so fuckin' good."

She bares her throat and I lift her thighs with my hands, opening her wide and give her what we both want.

By the end we're both streaked in a kaleidoscope of color and I can't help but think of the stripes of colors as a brand.

But not on her.

On me.

CHAPTER THIRTEEN

PEYTON

It's a sad, sad day when you wake up in bed after a night of glorious sex and realize it was a terrible mistake. I slap a hand over my eyes to ward off the blinding sunlight, but not before I get a glimpse of the naked man in bed beside me.

The incredibly muscular naked man in bed beside me.

Seriously, I didn't know a guy could have so many muscles.

I brave the sunlight and lose a good ten minutes just staring at the plump curve of his ass. Despite the headache pounding behind my eyes and the self-doubt roaring between my ears, I wonder if I shouldn't rouse him for another round, just for posterity's sake. Based on the soreness in my own body and the satisfied throb between my legs, he was entirely worth the inevitable morning-after awkwardness.

As I'm debating if I should smother myself with the pillow or risk inching out from underneath his grasp, Ford lets out a groan and the arm that's slung over my waist shifts off, freeing me. Carefully, so as not to wake him, I slip off the side and stumble to my feet. Clothes are scattered haphazardly over the floor and I can only find my flannel button up, so I slip my arms into it and begin to investigate the top floor in search of a bathroom. I seem to remember one at some point, but the memories are hazy. Triple X-rated, but hazy.

Once I'm in the hallway off the main space, I let out a breath and say to myself, "What the hell did you get yourself into, Peyton?"

The open concept living area where Ford and I had painted the night before leads down to a hallway with several closed doors, including the one I'd just escaped where Ford still snores softly. I peer into each closed door and find rooms in various states of disrepair until finally coming to a bathroom at the end of the hall. I test the water, the toilet, and give a small prayer of thanks that they're still working.

My reflection stares back at me accusingly in the mirror over the sink the second I flip the switch. I hadn't meant to let anything like last night happen. I sink onto the toilet and bury my face in my hands. Too much wine. Too much wine and not enough self-control. I don't know how to face him.

Even thinking about it has me shaking. It could be the worn out muscles in my thighs protesting as I flush and get back to my feet, but the twisting sensation in my belly isn't a result of the alcoholic overindulgence.

After washing my hands, I peer down the hallway, but there was not a peep coming from the bedroom. Must be quite the heavy sleeper. As I tiptoe past the doorway, I wonder how long I should let him snooze before I corner him for a very adult conversation. Not that I didn't enjoy our late-night aerobics, but I have no plans on scheduling a repeat. We just needed to let lose some steam, that was all.

I retrieve the rest of my clothes without waking him and decide to take a shower. Hopefully by then, Ford will be awake and as eager to put this night behind us as I am. He certainly doesn't seem like the commitment type and we both know I'm only staying in town long enough to figure out what happened to the woman on the lake and then I'm gone.

In order to save time, I straighten up all of my supplies while Ford is still asleep and stuff them into grocery store bags I find under the kitchen sink. With my clothes in hand, I silently inch my way toward the bathroom for that shower. I'm halfway down the hall when I hear the tell-tale sound of the toilet flush just feet away.

Damn the guy is quiet. I didn't even hear him get out of bed. He's not a small guy. You'd think he'd give a girl a warning. A squeaky floorboard or something, but no. As I learned last night he's got magnificent control of his muscular frame.

Even though I'm no stranger to the one-night-stand, my heart does a little shimmy and my stomach threatens to reject the remains of dinner still sloshing around inside it. After all, the sex was *really* good. If I had time to have a personal life, he'd be at the top of the list for an around the clock lover. He sure has the stamina for it.

With that in mind, I lean against the wall until the bathroom door opens and holy shit does he look better in full daylight. I'm into fitness, but this guy practically has abs on his abs and damn if his shoulders don't make me want to climb right on him and go for another ride.

"Mornin'," Ford says as he scratches his head. He stifles a yawn, then grins. Warmth stirs in my belly and I forget the reasons why I should be pushing him toward the nearest exit. "Sorry, had a late night."

My own responding smile feels decidedly feline in spite of my earlier determination to get as far away from him as fast as possible. "Yes, you did." I consider the way his unbuttoned jeans droop around his hips, decide to hell with it, and then I say, "Want a shower?"

Ford's grin darkens and a hand shoots out, quick as a snake, to capture my waist and jerk me against his hard body. My eyes zero in on the ink on his chest that I didn't notice the night before. I have an urgent need to trace it with my tongue...along with other parts of his body. It seems one taste of him wasn't enough.

One more, I decide. One more and then we'll forget it all.

I crowd him, angling us both back to the bathroom, my shirt slipping off my shoulders as we go. His lips find the sensitive skin there and I flick back the curtain and turn on the water as his hands palm my ass.

Screw reality, it can wait another hour...or two.

My body comes alive under his touch in a way that it hasn't in nearly three years. I moan against his lips and clutch at the material of his shirt to pull him closer. His body crashes into mine and I fall back against my car. He cages me there, his arms cradling my spine as though to protect it from any discomfort. But it doesn't matter. I can't feel anything but the pleasure his touch inspires.

"God," he says against my lips, then continues whispering against my throat, "I can't get enough of you. I thought I could, last night, but I was wrong. When I saw you this morning, all I could think about was touching you again, tasting you, taking you. You're driving me crazy, Peyton."

"We have to stop," I whisper back into the ether. The

words dissolve into the darkness, almost like I never said them. I'm not sure if I'm afraid that they're real or that I've only spoken them in my head.

"Don't say that now," he answers in a strangled voice. His heart thumps wildly under my palms and his breath is choppy and rapid. "If it weren't for Lexie, I'd drag you back inside and not let you go until tomorrow morning."

I strain against him, fears and doubts forgotten and drag his mouth back to mine. "I have to go," I say against his lips. "I've got to meet Alice to get the keys to my new place."

He chuckles and his hand trails down to cup my butt and press me against his hardness. Heat spikes through me and I moan. How is this guy human? "You sure about that?" he asks.

"Maybe not."

Then I get frustrated with talking and strain against him, cupping his face with both of my hands until the kiss turns needy and violent, all tongues and teeth knocking together, and urgency. I could kiss him forever and very nearly do until he breaks away, taking his hands from where they'd been kneading my ass and placing them on the car on either side of me. The sound of his breaths fill my ears as we both try to regain control.

"When can I see you again?" he asks, but he doesn't touch me. Which is probably for the best. A few seconds more and I would have begged him to take me right there in front of God and everyone.

God, get it together Peyton.

"Um," I say, trying to marshal my thoughts into some semblance of order. "That probably isn't a good idea."

He presses his forehead against my shoulder and dares to skim his hands up and down my back. "Are you fucking kidding me? It's the best idea I've had in years."

That steals a laugh from me and he lifts his head long enough to give me a devastating grin. If my knees weren't already weak, that smile would have done it. I lift a hand to his cheek and kiss him one last time. All at once, the way he makes me want to sigh in contentment also makes me want to run. The comfort is both seductive and terrifying.

With a shaky breath, I say, "This was nice, but you and I both know it isn't smart for it to become a thing."

Hands still caressing my back, he puffs out a sigh. "Yeah, I know. But it was sure fun."

"Maybe," I say, my voice wistful, "Maybe if things were different, but I've got a lot going on personally and I'm not in a place for a relationship. Besides, there's a lot I still don't know about you, and if I'm being honest, great sex aside, there's something about you that sort of scares me."

"Fair enough. But you can call me anytime, yeah? Since you're staying for a while, just because we can't do the relationship deal doesn't mean we can't be friends."

I nod, but I've already made up my mind not to see or talk to him more than I have to. As much as I want to tell myself it was just sex, there is nothing simple about Ford. A clean break is best, for both of us.

"I'd say you can call me if you run into any trouble, but trouble seems to find you and I probably shouldn't jinx it," he says.

When my smile threatens to wobble, I give him one last, long squeeze, then turn so he can't see how hard it is for me to walk away.

He waits on the sidewalk by his front door as I carefully buckle myself into my car and back out of his driveway. As I drive away he lifts a hand and I reply in kind, but the whole way home I have to wonder if I'm making some sort of colossal mistake. Not the sex, like I thought it was, but walking away.

CHAPTER FOURTEEN
FORD

THREE DAYS later and I still can't get Peyton out of my skull. I'd like to think that's why, as I drive away from my latest doctor's appointment, I can't seem to shake my splitting headache. I grumble underneath my breath as I navigate through traffic with Lexie, who Mercy neglected to mention needed a babysitter while she was off doing god-knows-what.

"Do you always cuss like that?"

I grit my teeth to keep from doing just that. "Like what?"

Lexie repeats some of my choicer words and I scowl. I'm such a great influence. It's easy to forget she's not one of the guys when I'm relaxed. I haven't had much experience around kids, but even I know foul language is probably a no-no. "Don't let your momma hear you talking like that."

"She wouldn't care," Lexie says and crosses her arms over her chest. "She doesn't care about anything but her boyfriends. She wouldn't even notice if I disappeared."

Dear God, save me from teenage girls. And clueless sisters. Sometimes I miss the desert where my problems were actual minefields instead of the metaphorical female kind. "You know she would. And if that doesn't matter to you, I'm here, I would."

Lexie snorts. "Yeah, right."

My head twinges and I regret not taking my doctor up on those pain meds he said were a dream for TBI's. It hasn't even been five minutes since the appointment and I'm already feeling tense. "What? You don't think I care about you?"

"C'mon, Uncle Ford, we barely see each other and even when we do, you act like you can't wait to leave," she says with her forehead pressed against the truck window.

"Look, kid, just because I'm not the talkative type doesn't mean that I don't care about you. You're family. All I know is if your mother or grandmother heard you swearin' up a storm like that, they'd have *my* hide. So just do me a favor and give me a break for once, please? If not, just put me out of my misery."

I don't have to look at her to know she's rolling her eyes at me.

"What happened to you?" she asks. "Why do you have to go to the doctor."

I groan mentally. "I got hurt," I say, missing the days when she had been a baby and the most noise she made was cooing or crying.

"How?"

Glancing over at her, I ruffle her hair and she squeals. "You know you ask a lot of questions?"

"You know you don't answer a lot of questions?" she shoots back.

The smirk I'd been wearing falls and I scowl. "You're a real pain in the ass, you know that?"

"Guess it runs in the family."

I can't help it, I laugh. "You're just like your mom, I swear to God."

"She says I'm just like you." She smiles, but she doesn't let up. "So what happened to you?"

I've long since gotten used to that question. "My unit was attacked last year. Have you ever heard of explosives?"

Her face grows serious. "I think so. Like on T.V.?"

"Sort of. Well anyway, the bad guys were shooting at my unit. When the mortars exploded, then caused a Traumatic Brain Injury or TBI."

"You hurt your brain?" she repeats, her voice going higher at the end. "How come I didn't know about this? Are you okay?"

"You're regretting giving me such a hard time now, aren't you?"

"Not a chance," she says, smiling. Then she repeats, "Are you going to be okay?"

"I'm gonna be fine, kid. It's not like I haven't been hurt before."

"You've been shot at *more than once*?" she squeals and I realize maybe I should have kept that little piece of information to myself.

So there goes the whole ride home. Not that I mind, really. It keeps me from being inside my own head too much. And Lexie isn't all that bad. In fact, she's a pretty good kid when she isn't being a brat, which isn't often. I guess if I'd been raised with a mother like Mercy, I'd be a brat, too. She and I are gonna have to have a long talk someday. This poor girl doesn't deserve to be shoved off on any willing family member so her mom can gallivant around with every available douchebag.

In fact, I think as I pull back up to the lodge, that's the first thing I'm gonna do before I check in with Nell. The lodge can wait. I glance over at Lexie who, I'll be damned, does look a little like me if I squint just right. Mercy has a lot of shaping up to do.

"You go inside and head to the main kitchens and snag something for lunch to eat. I'm gonna go find your mom and have a little chat."

Lexie pauses before opening her door, her eyes wide. "You aren't gonna tell her I cussed are you?"

I laugh. "No, honey, I won't tell her, I promise. Now go on."

The furor from the police search had died down and operations had gotten back to normal. I'm grateful as I stride through the front door that we haven't had anyone questioning about what happened. If I'm ever going to finish the upstairs renovations so I can release the rooms I'm using for myself to be booked, then I've got to keep booking percentages high. Even though I believe Peyton about what happened, part of me hopes the woman is never found for my own selfish reasons.

Nell looks up from the front desk. "Welcome back," she says.

"Everything good?"

"Quiet as a church," she replies.

"Have you seen my sister?" I ask.

"Not a peep. She must be busy."

Oh, I'll bet she is, I think as I head to my rooms. I can only hope she hasn't snuck in whatever loser she's currently seeing. But the living room is empty when I open the door.

"Mercy?" I call out. God knows, I don't want to find her twisted up somewhere half naked with some dude going at her. I'd rather dig my eyes out with a spoon. "Mercedes!"

She isn't in her room or the bathroom either. I curse

underneath my breath and dig out my phone. She answers on the third ring.

"I was just about to call you," Mercy says breathlessly over roaring wind.

"Where are you?" A motorcycle revs through the line and I have to count to three to keep from shouting. My headache kicks up a notch as foreboding causes my stomach to clamp down around the sandwich I'd had for lunch. "Mercy, where the fuck are you?"

"Don't be mad," she says.

"You only say that when you've done some shit that you know is gonna make me mad. Now, you're daughter is worried that you don't care about her. You're *not here* and I want you to tell me where you are."

Murmured conversation sounds over the phone line and I pace back and forth through the living room to keep from going off on her.

The revving motorcycle quiets, followed by static, and then Mercy saying, "I'm with a new friend of mine, we're goin' out of town for a couple days. I need you to watch Lexie for me, but don't worry, she's a good kid and she can take care of herself. Since that whole thing with the woman on the boat is over with, she'll be safe there with you. I promise it'll only be a couple days, a week at the most." I've been through a lot, but my mind goes perfectly blank at the thought of taking care of a teenage girl by myself for an entire week. At a loss for words, I can only rub at my eyes as Mercy continues. "She goes to school online so all you have to do is make sure she does her assignments on time and don't let her watch too much T.V.."

"You can't seriously be leaving her here with me to run off with some guy," I say very quietly, very calmly into the phone.

"C'mon, Ford, don't be a wet blanket. It's only for a couple of days and she can practically take care of herself. Look, I've gotta go. I'll call you when I'm heading back that way!"

She disconnects the call before I can say anything else.

"Uncle Ford? Is something wrong?"

I turn to the entryway and find Lexie standing there with two plates full of stuffed bell peppers and rice. She'd gotten me a plate and I hadn't even asked for it. For some reason, the gesture touches me. I put my phone back into my pocket and help her with the plate. She takes the seat next to me at the little counter bar.

"No, everything's fine. Thanks for bringing me a plate kiddo, I'm starving. It smells good."

Lexie nods, her face solemn. "Was that mom on the phone?"

The flavorful rice turns to chalk in my mouth. "Yeah, kiddo, it was."

She sighs. "What did she say?"

Damn you, Mercy. "I told her to take off for a couple days and stay out of our hair. She's been driving me crazy and I figured she hasn't been much better with you." The lies roll off my tongue with practiced ease. The poor kid thought her mom didn't want her. I couldn't let her know Mercy had left without a second thought.

Lexie's brightens a little. "You did?"

At her reaction, I know I made the right choice. "Well you're the one who says we barely know each other. This will give us the perfect opportunity." I nearly choke on the words, and for some reason Peyton comes to mind. For someone who didn't want shit to do with anyone, I'm putting down those roots left and right for all the females who won't leave well enough alone.

"Are you sure, Uncle Ford? Maybe we should call her and tell her to come back."

I get to my feet and get us both cokes from the mini fridge. "Now I'm insulted. I thought you'd like getting free run of the place."

"You mean I can do whatever I want?" she asks with a squeal.

"I didn't say that, but yes, if you can show me you're responsible with your schoolwork and help out around here if I need you to, I don't see why you won't be allowed certain freedoms." The words come so naturally they surprise me.

She rolls her eyes about the schoolwork, but seems pleased with the rest. "Do you think I can go hiking around the lake by myself?"

I think of the woman on the boat with a stirring of unease. "We'll see. I'll have to teach you some basic safety measures before you're allowed to go anywhere by yourself, but I'll consider it."

Lexie stuffs her face with a healthy forkful. "Cool," she says around the bite.

"Now eat and then I'll give you a tour of the grounds and teach you how to pull your weight." I barely keep from wincing at the tone in my voice. I remember my father saying something damn near identical to me when I was younger.

Fuckin' Mercy.

The whole reason I wanted the lodge was because it's smack dab in the middle of nowhere. I was supposed to live the rest of my days in relative peace and solitude. Instead I've got a nosy receptionist, a feisty niece, a hair-brained sister, and a bombshell blonde all working together to make sure I never have another moment's peace.

One week, I remind myself. One week and then they'll all be out of my hair and everything will go back to normal.

THE WEEKEND BROUGHT with it new tourists, families with children eager to make messes, wives with bottles of wine and cheery friends, and church socials with lots of laughter. The bustle keeps me so busy, I barely have time to think about the woman on the boat, let alone get back to the lake for another look. Whenever I think I have a moment to spare, Alice calls me back with another task.

Maybe after tonight's Art and W(h)ine event, I'll be able to sneak off to Bear Lake and give it a quick walk-around. No one has seen anything in the days since I left the lodge, but it's still cold out. There aren't that many people eager to brave the chill in the air for the views.

"Tourists prefer to see the views from the comfort of their toasty rooms," Alice says, walking over to the table to help clean up after a party of five.

"I'm sorry?"

"You were talking to yourself. About the weather, I think."

I blush as I wipe down the tables. "I'm sorry."

Alice grins and wipes her hands on an already paint-streaked apron. "Don't worry about it. We're all a little crazy."

Pausing, I wipe my hand across my forehead. "I'm sorry. I don't mean to complain. I guess you've probably heard what happened."

"There were rumors. I've heard you witnessed a murder!" She said it in that small town way where people don't want to be interested in something horrendous, but clearly are.

"Sometimes it feels like a nightmare instead of reality."

"They also said your parents were killed and you were there. That must make it awful hard for you to go through something like this again."

She isn't wrong. "I understand if you don't need more drama here. I promise I'll do my job and won't bring any trouble."

"You don't have to apologize to anyone, least of all me. I've never seen anything like that and I wouldn't begin to know how you're feeling. The best medicine is to keep yourself busy."

"Well, you've certainly been helping with that," I tell her, smiling to take the edge off the remark.

"You've been a wonderful help. We've just got the last party today and then I'll let you go for the afternoon. You deserve a break after all the hard work you've been doing."

I stow away the paints on the cart. "You don't have to do that. I'm grateful for the work."

Alice makes a sound in her throat. "Don't go contradicting me now. Get this cleaned up and the party room prepped, then you can clock out. I know you've got some work to do at your apartment anyway."

She wasn't wrong. In exchange for a break on the rent, Alice was allowing me to fix up the place piece by piece. A coat of paint here, some cleaning there. I didn't mind the extra work because she was right, it did keep me busy. You couldn't worry if you didn't have time to stop long enough to do it.

"Thank you, Alice, you can't know how much I appreciate it."

"No need to thank me. Don't forget to take out the trash."

AN HOUR LATER, AS I PULL UP THE DRIVE TO THE little house Alice had graciously rented out to me, I know I won't be able to get out to the lake before dark. Not when my feet are screaming and my eyes are so gritty I can barely see straight. For such a small town, Alice's little shop is sure doing brisk business.

I heft my purse onto my shoulder with a can of mace in one hand and the keys to the house in the other. I leave the porch light on all day and night, just in case, and the halo of yellow light comforts me as I ascend the steps.

My heart tumbles to my feet and my stomach jerks like it's been hooked by a fisherman when the door to the house comes open as smooth as silk at a brush from my hand. Frozen in place, I try to remember my steps from that morning. I could have sworn I locked it. It's not like me to leave without triple checking the locks, and then once more for good measure. My ears strain at the crack in the door to listen.

I don't know whether I should turn and run or dig in my purse for my phone and the fact that I should know better brings frustrated tears to my eyes. When my fingers can move, I go for my phone first as quietly as possible. I key in 9-1-1 and then push open the door with my foot. The resulting squeal from the hinges sends spiders crawling up and down my spine.

The house is such that I can see straight through to the back door with an open kitchen and living room area. The two small bedrooms and bath are off to my right, the doors open and the interiors beyond bright and sunny with afternoon light. I take a careful step forward and flip on the hallway and living room lights.

I don't know if I should be relieved there are no sinister shadows or even more worried. Had I really forgotten to double check the locks? Was I that distracted? I carry my phone and the can of mace through every room, my heart still thundering in my chest even when I confirm the house is empty save for me.

After I lock and bolt the door, check all the windows, and do the same to the back door, I then go through all my things. It's a precaution, probably a useless one, but I won't be able to settle until I've looked at everything and then looked at it again.

When I finish the living room, kitchen, and bathroom, I go to my room. It's the larger of the two, if you're being generous and manages to fit a full sized bed with a night stand and skinny dresser. Because of the frantic schedule at work I haven't had the chance to unpack yet so I go to the closet where I've stowed my suitcase.

I nearly crash into the floor when my feet go out from under me. I manage to catch myself on the door frame, knocking my wrists and bruising my knuckles in the process. Once I'm steady, I carefully get to my feet and pull the cord for the closet light.

For a moment, I think I'm seeing things because I'm so tired and my nerves are shot from the adrenaline of finding the door open. But after opening and closing my eyes, the scene in front of me doesn't change.

Water drips from my suitcase and onto the floor in a puddle that had caused me to slip on the worn linoleum. I can barely manage a breath as I reach out a tentative hand for the zipper. I'm half expecting to find the body of the woman inside, broken and crumpled to fit. Instead, when I unzip a wet ball of clothes tumbles from the interior and lands at my feet in a wet *plop*.

It's the clothes I was wearing the night I saw the woman being murdered. My brows furrow as I fall to my knees to study them. It can't be right. It can't be. But I open them up and spread them across the floor. It's the same shirt, the same jeans. Except, I'd had them laundered that night because I couldn't bear to look at them. I'd stored them in the dry-cleaning bags because I wasn't sure I could wear them again.

I paw through the closet, but the hangers and the dry cleaning bags are gone. I could have sworn it was the only thing I had hung in the closet. Could I have forgotten? The moldy, earthy smell of damp clothes soaked in lake water wafts up to my nose. The scent is undeniable. It even smells like that night.

Fumbling, I paw at the clothes and roll them into a saturated ball. The water soaks into my apron and jeans, but I can barely feel the chill. I make my way, nearly stumbling, to the kitchen where I throw the clothes into the garbage can and slam the lid shut.

I must have been mistaken. That's the only logical explanation. I've lost time before, forgotten how I spent the day or misremembered events. It hasn't happened in a long time and I thought I'd gotten past it, but maybe the stress of losing the money, of witnessing the murder had brought all those feelings back up.

Even so, I shower with the curtain open, water going everywhere, but I don't care. The thought of being vulnerable in any capacity has me on edge for the rest of the evening. I can barely choke down my dinner and because sleeping is an impossibility, I stay up nearly all night trying, and failing, to paint again.

In the first light of dawn, I'm nodding off in the big, old two-seater chair when a knock at the door brings me to my feet and the cup of tea I'd been holding crashing to the floor. I fly to the door, heedless of the shattered china, and wish I'd brought a gun instead of the can of mace. I peer through the lace curtains on the peekaboo window and find a man's face on the other side.

I nearly rip the door off its hinges as I swing it open, relief turning my legs into jello. "Uncle Brad!"

His mouth twitches under a thick silver beard. "Hey there, peanut."

I launch myself into his arms, thankful for their

comforting weight around me. "What are you doing here?"

"You didn't think I'd let you run all over the country without checking on you did you? I know you wanted to do this on your own, but you have to give an old man a break."

Normally, I'd be furious he followed me, but right now, I could use the reassurance. "Don't be silly. I'm happy you're here." I tug him inside and shut the door behind him. "How long will you be able to stay?"

"Just a couple days. Did something happen?" he asks.

I blink a few times. Surely he can't read my expression that easily? "W-what?"

He gestures to the broken china. "You hurt yourself?"

Relieved, I get to my knees and start picking up the mug. "No, you startled me is all. Honestly, I was half asleep in the chair when you knocked and the cup went flying from my hands. It's nothing, I promise."

Uncle Brad takes a seat opposite me on the loveseat. "Nothing, huh? You sure about that?"

I put the cup in the trash and grab a hand towel to soak up the liquid. "What do you mean?"

"Come on, peanut. I know you better than that. I heard on the news that someone witnessed a murder here. A young woman with long blonde hair. An artist."

I wince. "I was hoping you wouldn't find out about that."

"Why didn't you tell me?" he asks and I can't look up

from the floor where I mop up the mess.

"I didn't want you to worry."

His sigh makes my heart heavy. "It's the not knowing that worries me more than anything. You've already been through more than enough for one lifetime. You shouldn't have to go through these things alone."

I send him a sunny smile. "You don't have to worry. I've spoken with the Sheriff, they're doing everything they can. It may have just been a huge misunderstanding."

"Do you really think so?"

"Uncle Brad, I appreciate you coming, but you don't need to worry. The people here have been very kind to me. I've got a wonderful job, this place. I'm safe here."

"So safe you witnessed a murder?"

"There's no evidence so far a murder was ever committed." The words taste like acid on my tongue. But I choke them out because being smothered once again is worse than thinking I imagined it all.

"Be that as it may, I hope you don't mind if I stay a couple days."

I paste on a cheery smile. "Of course not!"

Having Uncle Brad over cements the decision in my mind not to report the door unlocked or the wet clothes to the Sheriff. It was probably nothing, anyway.

Maybe the stress of the past week had finally gotten to me.

As THE WEEK turns into the weekend, it's made very clear I know nothing about kids, especially teenagers, but with Nell's help, we manage. It isn't pretty, but she's alive, so I consider it a job well done.

"Do you mind watching her for a couple hours? I want to take a walk around the lake." I ask Nell when business slows down Sunday morning.

"I'm not a baby," Lexie interrupts. "I don't need a babysitter."

"You're not getting free reign of the lodge, either," I tell her, then to Nell, I say, "If she gives you any trouble, there's some rope in the shed. Just tie her up and leave her until I get back."

Nells eyes sparkle. "You leave it to me. We'll have a girls' night."

"Just don't burn the place down. Play nice with Nell," I tell Lexie.

"When is mom coming home?" Lexie asks. She signs and rolls her eyes, but I can tell her mother's absence is bothering her. Damn Mercy. Much as Lexie is trying to cover up how much it bothers her, there's no hiding the hurt in her gaze.

I've been trying to call Mercy all week. When she did answer, she gave me every excuse in the book. She'll be back in a couple days. Money trouble. Car trouble. Excuse after excuse. The truth is, I don't have any answers for Lexie and I'm not going to give her an excuse. I don't want to lie to her. I may lie to everyone else, including myself, but I won't lie to her.

"I don't know, sweetheart, but until she gets back she left me in charge and I say you're going to hang out with Nell for a little while."

Lexie bites her lip. "You're coming back right?"

I pause at the door and turn back. "Of course I am. We'll binge something when I get back--your choice."

That causes her to smile. "You promise?"

Remembering something Mercy and I used to do when we were children, I lean across the counter, extending my hand. "Pinky promise."

Lexie rolls her eyes again, but she wraps her pinky finger around mine.

THE QUIET WRAPS AROUND ME LIKE A LOVER AND I feel a little guilty for how much I'm enjoying being alone as I travel deeper and deeper into the forest. I don't have to take the long way around to get to the opposite side of the lake to begin my search, but after a week of dealing with Lexie's teenage angst and Mercy's absenteeism, I'm remembering why I used to enjoy deployments so goddamn much.

Sheriff Hadley has all but written Peyton's reports off, but there's a nagging feeling in the pit of my stomach that won't let me do the same. I keep coming back to seeing Peyton floating in the water, lifeless. If I had any sense at all, I'd forget the whole thing and go back to being the grouchy recluse, but it's the not knowing that's making me edgy. At first I wanted it all to go away. For everyone and everything to leave me alone so I could stew in my own misery. I still want that, but as long as I've got Peyton hovering around trying to figure out what happened, I can kiss my so-called peace good-bye.

I may not find anything today, but the last thing I need is for Peyton to decide to play detective and traipse all over Windy Point looking for a murderer. I've had blood on my hands enough in my lifetime--I don't want to add hers to it.

With that in mind, I aim toward the shoreline, leaving my sanctuary behind me. We'd had a storm come through a couple days back and the rain should have churned up any secrets that may or may not lay at the bottom of Bear Lake. Any evidence left from the assault may have washed ashore in the meantime and this may be my only chance to figure out what happened once and for all.

I weave through a break in the trees and find a lone figure marching along the beach. At first, I scowl, thinking maybe Lexie followed me down after all, then I get closer and there's no mistaking the whip of golden hair or the lush ass and pert breasts. My mouth goes dry remembering what those pretty rose-brown nipples taste like. Knowing I can't go there again only pushes me from annoyed to pissed off.

"You're just asking for trouble, aren't you?" I say, when I get close enough that she'll hear me over the roaring wind.

At my voice, she spins and it takes a moment for her eyes to focus in on me. "I really hate that saying," she says instead of answering. "Who actually asks for trouble? It's insulting."

Marching forward, I take her arm in my grasp. Damn woman shouldn't be walking out here on her own. "You shouldn't be here by yourself. You know good and well if there is someone killing people in Windy Point they've heard that you're the one who witnessed the murder by now. You realize that makes you a target?"

She jerks her arm from my grasp and stumbles back like she can't get far enough away from me. "And you should realize that no matter what I do, I can't stop someone who doesn't operate by a moral code of any sort. It wouldn't matter if I was alone or not if they did want to target me. You of all people should know that."

She's going to be the death of me. "What are you doing out here?"

"I'm working on my tan. What do you think I'm doing? I take back what I said. You must be crazy."

Her eyes go wild. "I spent a long time trapped in my own house, in my own mind. I've been crazy before so that doesn't offend me."

"Good, 'cause I meant it as a fuckin' compliment. Now are you going to come with me to look around or are we going to spend the next couple hours arguing? There's only so much daylight."

"Why do you have to irritate me so much?" she asks as we begin walking. "You would have thought the sex would have softened you up some."

I snort. "It'd take a lot more than one night to soften me up."

When she falls silent, I begin to think I've offended her. Mentally berating myself, I try to come up with an appropriate apology. This is what happens when you spend the majority of your adult life surrounded by men with nothing but time on your hands.

Before I can, she says, "Thank you," so quietly I almost wonder if I've imagined it.

"You're welcome?"

She stuns me by grinning. "You don't ever treat me like I'm broken. I think I got so used to people coddling me, my uncle, friends, people I used to know, my therapist. It's refreshing to have someone who just doesn't give a damn about how messed up in the head I am."

"We're all a little broken, Peyton."

"Are you ever going to tell me what parts of you are broken? I've shared my scars, it only seems fair," she says.

Isolated the way we are by the sound of the wind rustling the bare bones of the trees and the lap of waves against the sand, it's almost easy to open up to her. "I'm an open book."

"You're a concrete wall."

"Let's work on tackling your demons before we start in on mine," I suggest.

"I wouldn't even know where to start now. My plan pretty much stopped at getting down here and looking around."

I smirk. "We're going to walk around the lake and look around."

"Of course we are," she says.

The silence is unbearable so I find myself saying, "What happened to the people who hurt you?" The thought of someone putting their hands on her, terrifying her is unthinkable. My hands clench by my sides.

"The police tried looking for them, at first, but there wasn't much to go on. Three men in ski masks. Guns. White sneakers is what I remembered most vividly."

"What happened?"

Peyton kicks at a leaf, then picks up a rock and throws it into the lake. It lands with a satisfying plop. "The three of us were at home one random Tuesday. It was late and we were watching a show on T.V. when our dog, Lady, started going crazy at the back door. She was a Lab and could be high strung, so we didn't think too much of it at the time. When she wouldn't stop barking, I went to let her out." Her breath shudders out of her. I don't know if she notices, but as she talks, she's gesturing wildly and talking faster. "There was just one of them at first. He came out of nowhere. One second, I was holding onto Lady and the next he had me by the throat against a wall. I didn't even have the chance to scream, to warn my parents."

"Times moves faster when shit starts happening."

"Was it like that for you?" she asks.

"Sometimes. Sometimes it's fast." I look out into the distance. "Others it's like it stops, freezes. What happened next?"

"That makes sense," Peyton says absently. "The one who grabbed me took me down to the basement. I could hear him talking to others, but I didn't get a real good look at them. As he was pushing me down the stairs, I heard my mom scream. My dad was shouting. They didn't stop for a long time. And then they were quiet, real quiet. I almost wished I could hear them screaming and shouting again because it would mean they were alive."

"What did they want?"

"Money, of course. Nothing more and nothing less. We lived in an affluent part of town. My parents were both from well-off families. The police told us they'd stalked us for a couple days to figure out which houses would be the easiest to get into. They were right. I didn't put up much of a fight and my parents paid with their lives."

"Bullshit," I say.

She stops so abruptly her shoes kick up sand. "What?"

"C'mon, Peyton, that's bullshit and you know it. There's no way you can fight off three armed men and survive. You're lucky you got out of there with your life."

"Lucky," she says sardonically. "I'm not sure I'd consider it lucky. For a while all I could think about was that I couldn't do anything to save them. That they deserved to live because they were great people, wonderful parents. It should have been me."

"But it wasn't."

She glares at me. "I'm going to remind you of this when I

pry out what happened to you to make you such a sweetheart."

"Bring it on."

"Now you said you saw the boat more toward this side of the lake, opposite the dock at the lodge." I point in the direction.

"Thereabouts, it's hard to be absolutely certain. Things are a little hazy now after knocking myself on the head." She pauses, then puts a hand on my arm to stop me.

"What is it? Did you remember something?"

"No, but there is something I feel like I should tell you before I drag you any farther into this. You know me, what I've been through. I've been absolutely honest with you about everything."

"A first from a woman, in my experience," I say, thinking of Mercy abandoning Lexie.

"Then I have to tell you, I came home from working at Splatters yesterday and found my clothes from the night I fell in the lake. They were all soaked."

"So, what?"

"I could have sworn I'd had them cleaned. But they were so wet there was a puddle underneath them." Her brows furrow and she bites her lip. "You may have been joking about me going off the rails, but I'm starting to think maybe I hit my head harder than I thought."

"Have you been forgetting other things? Losing time?

Having headaches?" Considering my own experience, I should know.

"Not that I know of, it's just so strange and I wanted you to know before you start this wild goose chase again."

"First thing tomorrow morning you're going into the clinic and I don't want to hear any argument about it."

"I don't want to see more doctors, Ford. I've seen enough for a lifetime."

I can sympathize. "Too bad. I'll drag you there myself if I have to."

She changes the subject, but I make a mental note to get up early and waylay her before she can evade me. I have to admit, the way she constantly challenges me is going against every natural instinct I have to stay away from her.

"Did Hadley figure out if there were any boats seen that night?"

"He asked around, but no one owned up to it if there were. No boats missing, either."

"So it would have to be someone from the area, maybe, who knows the lake, how to get in and out quickly without being seen."

When she glances over at me, I smirk. "My boat was in the slip all night. I've got security footage to prove it."

Her responding flirtatious smile knocks every sensible thought out of my head. "Just checking." She lifts a hand to shade her eyes as she looks out over the water. "How many docks are there where a boat could get in and out?"

"A dozen or so, give or take one or two. There are houses all along the lake, the slips at the lodge for regulars. We don't get many this time of year. I checked and we didn't have any rentals the days before or after."

She drops her hands to her sides. "With as many officers as Hadley had patrolling the area, you'd have thought we'd know more by now."

"Unless the person you saw did a damn good job of covering it up."

My heart plummets to my feet. In the days since I'd witnessed the murder, it had never occurred to me they had seen me in return, at least not as viscerally as it does on the open bank with the cover of trees all around. Anyone could be out there, hiding, watching. Waiting.

"You're kidding, right?" I sputter out. "It was dark. They never looked up at me." Then I recall falling off the dock. Could he have heard me splashing into the water?

"With the way news spreads in this town, he probably knew that night. If not, then the next day for sure, especially if he was local."

"If you're trying to scare me, you're sure as hell doing a great job of it."

"It's about time you got scared. You need to be more

careful when you go out on your hikes. Bring someone with you."

"You think it's that serious?"

"I think if someone is going to the trouble of concealing a murder so well that the police can't find a sign and they knew you saw them, then they have to be worried about what else you may have seen."

"If you're right and they did cover their tracks, then that night, they must have taken the-the body with them. Hid it somewhere else to make sure the cops wouldn't find any evidence of it."

I stare out over the glassy surface of the lake and shiver. It hadn't occurred to me that night because of the shock of everything going on, but I'd been in that water with the woman when she lost her life. I'd been so close and couldn't save her. Just like I hadn't been able to save my parents. The dark depths seem much more ominous than they did the day I arrived in Windy Point. Even though I know her body more than likely isn't among the long, slimy arms of seaweed, their dancing shadows send fingers of fear up and down my spine.

"Then, the body could be anywhere. Lots of places for someone to get lost out here in the mountains. There are other rivers, lakes."

"That poor woman. No one to know where she went, or

even that she's missing. It's like she simply doesn't exist anymore."

Ford steps into my view, blocking the lake. "She does. You saw her, you know what happened. We'll do what we can to make sure we find out what he did with her."

"If he took her body away, we don't have the boat or any other sign of them, then all we have is my word to go on."

"I didn't take you for a cynic," Ford said as we began walking the rest of the way around the lake. "Shouldn't artists be all dreamy, hopeless romantic types?"

"I think anything dreamy and romantic about me died a long time ago," I reply with a wry smile.

"I wouldn't say so."

I give him an arched look. "Really? Why not?"

With his eyes on the shoreline in the steady, calculating way of his, Ford simply shrugs. "I looked up some of your work. You can't paint the way you do and say you aren't a romantic. I've seen people who've lost hope, lost the light inside them." He glances back at me, cool and assessing. "You aren't one of them."

"Well be still my heart, I think you just gave me a compliment."

He shrugs, the tips of his ears going a little pink. The sight delights me in ways that it shouldn't for someone who wants to keep her distance. "Don't go picking out rings over it."

"I wouldn't dream of it." Well, who'd have thought it? Ford has a soft side. I'd counseled myself out of wanting more than the one night with him, but damn if I don't wish circumstances were different. "I don't think we're going to find anything out here," I say, trying to distract myself from thoughts of his lips on mine again.

"It was a long shot."

"Yeah, probably, but I appreciate you taking the time to come look."

"Anytime. Let me walk you back up to your car."

I reach out and snag his jacket with a hand. "You don't have to do that."

The look he gives me has me releasing my hold. "I'm not going to let you wander around the woods by yourself. Don't make me throw you over my shoulder," he says. When my body heats and my nipples tighten, his eyes go right to the thin material of my shirt. My flimsy bra does nothing to hide my arousal. "Jesus," he murmurs. I don't know if it's an expletive or a plea.

When he steps closer, I don't think I care. All the rationalizing I'd done when I pushed him away evaporates as he pins me against a tree. He thrusts his hands into my hair and as much as I'm intimidated by his size, I realize there are some definite advantages as those wide palms and long fingers cradle and massage my scalp. He overwhelms me, undoes me. Even as his mouth covers mine, I know resistance is useless. Despite my fears, I submit to him, accept the dominant thrust of his tongue. Because when a man like Ford kisses you, it's not a seduction. It's an overtaking.

My body comes alive under his touch in a way that it hasn't in longer than I can remember. I moan against his lips and clutch at the material of his shirt to pull him closer. His body crashes into mine and I fall back against the tree, heedless of the bark biting into my flesh. He cages me there, his arms cradling my spine as though to protect it from any discomfort. But it doesn't matter. The second his hands dip beneath my shirt, I can't feel anything but the pleasure his touch inspires.

"God," he says against my lips, then continues whispering against my throat, "I can't get enough of you. I thought I could, that night, but I was wrong. When I saw you all I could think about was touching you again, tasting you, taking you. You're driving me crazy, Peyton."

"What if I said you could have me again?" I whisper back into the ether. The words dissolve into the darkness, almost like I never said them. I'm not sure if I'm afraid that they're real or that I've only spoken them in my head.

"Don't say that now," he answers in a strangled voice. His heart thumps wildly under my palms and his breath is choppy and rapid. "If it weren't for Lexie, I'd drag you back to my place and not let you go until tomorrow morning."

I strain against him, fears and doubts forgotten and drag

his mouth back to mine. "I can be quiet," I say against his lips.

He chuckles and his hand trails down to cup my butt and press me against his hardness. Heat spikes through me and I moan. "You sure about that?" he asks.

"Maybe not."

Then I get frustrated with talking and strain against him, cupping his face with both of my hands until the kiss turns needy and violent, all tongues and teeth knocking together, and urgency. I could kiss him forever and very nearly do until he breaks away, taking his hands where they'd been kneading my ass and placing them on the tree on either side of me. The sound of his breaths fill my ears as we both try to regain control.

"I don't give a fuck about if you're leaving or timing bull-shit. I want to see you again," he says, but he doesn't touch me. Which is probably for the best. A few seconds more and I would have begged him to take me right there in front of God and everyone.

God, get it together Peyton.

"Um," I say, trying to marshal my thoughts into some semblance of order. "Wait, what? I don't--"

"It's not rocket science, sunshine. Much as I want to get you naked, we should probably back up and do this the right way."

I shake my head to clear it. "The right way?"

"As in dinner, movies." He lifts a shoulder, skims his lips over mine. "A date."

My breath shudders out against his mouth. I pull back far enough to suck in gulps of cool air. "You're asking me out on a date."

He presses his forehead against my shoulder and skates his hands up and down my back. "Around five. That work for you? There are a couple places in town, I'm not picky so you can choose as long as it's not the vegan place. I like you well enough, but I need real food."

That steals a laugh from me and he lifts his head long enough to give me a devastating grin. If my knees weren't already weak, that smile would have done it. I lift a hand to his cheek and kiss him one last time. All at once the way he makes me want to sigh in contentment also makes me want to run. The comfort is both seductive and terrifying.

With a shaky breath, I say, "One date. I'm not promising anything other than that."

He tugs my hand and begins to walk. I'm assuming it's in the direction of where I parked, but even if my head weren't swimming from his kiss, I'd have no clue. "I don't need promises, Peyton. I just want you."

THE NEXT DAY I CAN BARELY KEEP FROM DANCING around the floor at work and am humming underneath my breath when Alice idles over and crosses her arms over her chest, an amused smile dancing on her lips. "Something's got you in a mighty fine mood," she says.

"I've got a date," I confide, unable to keep the news to myself. Uncle Brad isn't exactly one for gossip and I haven't had time to make many any other girlfriends.

"Oh, really? And who exactly is the lucky guy?"

I scoot forward in the chair at the table where I'm sorting through supplies. The chair legs squeal against the tiles, but I don't care. I have to tell someone before I burst wide open. "Ford. Ford Collier? From the lodge."

Instead of being excited, Alice leans forward, her voice growing serious. "Ford? Really?"

I ease back, her tone tamping down on my mood. "Yes. Why?"

She shrugs noncommittally and then waves at a couple of customers who are on their way out. "Just that nasty business when he was in the service and all. Didn't you hear about that?"

I recall my conversation with Lexie. "Of course. I haven't questioned him about it, we've barely spent much time together. This is technically our first date."

Alice gets to her feet and lays a hand on my shoulder. "I'm sure it's nothing, dear. What do you two plan on doing?"

My enthusiasm somewhat diminished, I concentrate on

putting lids on paint bottles and tubes. "Well, I'm not sure. He's been secretive about it. All I know is to meet him at the lodge today after work and to wear clothes I don't mind getting dirty. I think he's probably taking me hiking somewhere."

"Probably going to take you up to Windy Point. Have you been?"

"I haven't had the chance yet. I've been so busy with my Uncle coming into town and getting settled. I've heard it's beautiful, though."

"It's gorgeous. There are a ton of trails and it can be very romantic if you go up there right near sunset. Lots of inspiration."

"Sure sounds like it." I glance up at the clock, noting I still have another half-hour before the end of my shift. I can practically feel the ticking of the second-hand throughout my whole body.

"You look like you're about to jump out of your skin, girl."

I laugh at myself. "I know, I'm being silly. It's just that I haven't been on a date in a long time and even though he and I are sort of friends, I feel giddy. It's ridiculous, I'm sorry," I babble as I tote the supplies to the closet.

"You don't have to apologize to me. I've been married for the better part of two decades and you remind me of what my husband and I were like when we were your age."

"I shouldn't be going out with him since I don't know how long I'll be staying."

Alice puts a hand on her hip. "Now I may not be so keen on Ford in particular, considering his past, but you have a right to take your happiness while you can get it, God knows it can be in short supply." She catches me glancing at the clock again and her responding laugh is tinged with a bit of exasperation. "Oh, why don't you run along home? I know I won't get much done with you for the rest of the day with you distracted. Besides, you've worked hard this last week."

"Are you sure?" I ask as I start to undo my apron and grab my purse from my employee cubby.

I'm already half out the door when she answers. "You be careful now!"

Except, I'm barely listening. I think I'm done being careful. I left my old life so I could take chances. Life is short and I want to take a chance on Ford.

"But how come you get to go out on a date and I don't?" Lexie screeches as she follows me from my bedroom to the bathroom. "It's not fair!"

"Because I'm an adult and you're a child. You can date when you're thirty."

Lexie makes a disgusted face in the mirror, causing me to chuckle. "That's *ancient* Uncle Ford. Besides, Cody, the boy whose parents are staying in room 214 will only be here for a couple more days. He'll be ancient, too, by the time I'm thirty. He'll probably ask someone else if you say no."

I study Lexie in the mirror. "If you don't bug me for the rest of the night, I'll think about it and ask your mother when I get home." She begins to squeal and I give her a stern look. "I mean it, the rest of the night."

181

She nods her head almost violently. "Yes, I hear you, Uncle Ford. I won't make a peep. You won't hear me, you won't see me. I'll be like a little mouse."

"If your mom says no, then that's that and I don't want to hear any whining about it. Got it?"

Lexie's smile falls a little and she says, "It's not like she'll care. She's off having fun and she left me here. She shouldn't really even get a say."

Sometimes I forget the young woman behind me isn't the two year old with the raucous giggle and pigtails who used to chase me around the rare times I was able to come home on leave. She'd grown up on me, in more ways than one, and as she stares down at her hands, for the first time since they showed up on my doorstep, I'm grateful.

"Hey, look here." She glances up, then tries to look away, but I take her chin between my fingers. "Your mother has her problems, everyone does, even me, but she does love you. When she gets back she and I will have a serious conversation about leaving you like she did, but I want you to know that I care about you. I haven't said it near enough, but I'm here for you, even if she isn't."

Her eyes water, making me vaguely uncomfortable, then she throws herself bodily into my arms. "I love you, Uncle Ford," she says against my chest. "I'm glad you're here."

Lungs tight, I press a kiss to her hair and inhale the scent of strawberries. "I love you, too, squirt."

She squeezes again for emphasis, then bounds backwards a couple steps. "I'm going to go check outside and see if Peyton's got here yet. Maybe Cody is in the lobby!"

I follow her movement out of the bathroom with a smile tugging at my lips. I may not have been overjoyed to find her and my sister on my doorstep, but maybe the best things in life are sometimes the most unexpected.

Once I've finished getting ready, I grab my wallet and keys from the nightstand and find Lexie chattering animatedly with Peyton at the front door.

"Ready to go?" I ask when I reach them.

Peyton's eyes sparkle when they meet mine. "Sure." To Lexie, she says, "Next time you see him, make sure to make him work for it. You're a very special girl and sometimes guys need to work for it a little."

Lexie nods like Peyton's imparted the knowledge of the universe. "I will."

"You go to bed when Nell tells you and no more chasing boys for the night or I'll rescind my offer."

"Yes, sir, I promise."

Peyton wraps her arm around mine. "I'll take good care of him, I promise." Lexie's delighted giggles follow us out the door. "Boy troubles?" she asks.

"I guess. I'm going to throttle her mother when she gets back."

Her hand finds its way to my thigh and I realize I could get used to having her around all the time, having her touch me. I take her hand in mine as I begin to drive.

"What happened to her?"

"She ran off with some guy. Who knows? I'm hoping she'll be back soon because I don't know dick about taking care of kids."

"She's still alive, so you must be doing something right."

I snort. "That's setting the bar high. So what about you? Any kids or nieces and nephews?"

"No," she says with a laugh. "I was in no place to have children. I could barely take care of myself after my parents died let alone a child. My Uncle Brad, my mom's brother, is the only family I have left, actually. He's staying at my cabin with me for a couple days right now."

"Checking up on you?" I ask with a sideways glance.

"Something like that. He worries."

"Does he know about..."

"Yes, and that's why I don't want to worry him more than he already is. As much as I love him, I need my space now to live my life. If he had it his way I'd stay in his little perfectly controlled bubble where nothing could ever happen to me." I think of Lexie and if something were to ever happen to her, I'm not sure I'd react any differently than Peyton's uncle. Before I can say as much, she holds up a hand. "Don't even say it. I don't want to hurt you before we've even got to where we're going. Where are we going anyway? My boss Alice mentioned something about the real Windy Point?"

My thumb idly caresses her fingers and I decide I could absolutely get used to this. "We're going near there. Not quite up that high since it's your first time, but I thought you'd enjoy seeing the river out there, it feeds into the lake. Lots of great views and critters to see. I figured you wouldn't want to stay cooped up."

For some reason my words cause her to lean over and kiss my cheek. "Who knew inside such a grumpy exterior there's a big old softie."

Uncomfortably intrigued by the way her eyes shine up at me with something like affection, I say, "I'll remind you of that when we've been hiking in the woods for a couple hours and you're near eat up by mosquitos and starving."

But she isn't daunted. "It sounds divine," she says.

I take her up the highway toward Windy Point and veer off at a signage proclaiming it a historic landmark. We don't go all the way down the road, however, instead we turn off on a side road and park in the designated parking area. Even though we're not all the way up to the top of the mountain, the views are still spectacular. Thick, lush forests topping the peaks in every direction.

It stuns me to realize I already know her well enough to be certain she's thinking about how to best capture what's in front of us on canvas.

"I can't get over how beautiful it is here," she tells me as I gather our gear from the back and load it up. She shocks me by taking a pack of her own and shouldering it. "You're lucky I didn't bring any supplies or I'd keep you out here for days trying to capture this light alone."

"Sounds like heaven to me. I'd bring a couple beers and one of those hammocks and I'd be good to go." What I don't say is that I'd be more interested in watching her work than getting some shut eye. From what little I've seen of her at work, she's a sight to watch when she's distracted and intent upon whatever images in her mind she's trying to bring to life. If I'm being honest, I could watch her for hours.

I take her hand and lead her to a marked trail that disappears between the bases of large trees whose tops seem to brush the clouds. It's like being on the top of the world. For a woman who'd spent an eternity locked behind four walls and a roof, it must feel like flying—or at least, that's what I was going for.

Peyton's smiling, so I figure I'm on the right track. "Really? You wouldn't mind doing nothing out here while I worked?" She sounds shocked and then I remember she hasn't seen me at my best. Then again, who has in the past couple years.

"Babe, I spent hours sitting in a lookout in the middle of the desert with a lot less attractive view. Being out here with you, watching you work, seeing you happy in your element, I have to tell you that's no hardship." As soon as I say the words, I realize how right they feel and how much I want that in my life.

"Spoil me like that and I could get real used to it."

I glance back as we crest the first incline. Already my thighs are loose from the exertion and sweat lines my brow. Maybe it's the endorphins from the exercise, maybe it's the way she's smiling up at me again. I'm collecting those smiles like a miser. I want to keep them all to myself. "Maybe I'd want you to get used to it."

She makes a humming sound in the back of her throat. "You don't mind that I'm not really into the whole public dinner date thing? You seemed to know I'd prefer being outdoors like this, but I want to be sure. I want you to have a good time, too."

"Do I look like the kind of man who prefers fine dining over a burger?" I roll my shoulders and lead her up another crest. "Besides, I get twitchy in big crowds. The noise, the people. It makes me a bit claustrophobic. I prefer the mountains to the Met any day."

A half-hour or so later, we reach the destination I'd picked out, a cliff with a view of the river cutting through the rock in either direction. The moment she sees the view, she gasps and hurries to the ledge. She lifts her face up to the light and I know I picked the perfect place to let my caged bird fly.

I didn't plan on her, flat out didn't want her once I realized how much she'd gotten under my skin, but seeing the way she takes pleasure in the sunset reminds me of a life I thought I'd lost a long time ago.

At first I wanted nothing more than to lose myself in a body. Any body. But when we'd made love, she forced me to be present rather than drowning myself in her sweet oblivion. It was her eyes. Those big brown eyes so full of pain. She'd tried to hide it when I first met her, but I could see straight through her mile-wide grin to the agony she kept hidden underneath.

I recognized a piece of myself in her and I wanted to know more. Then after I had a taste of her, I knew I'd need another and another until it became a part of me.

When the light grows dark, I take her hand. "We'd better get back before we walk ourselves right off the cliff." She squeezes my hand in reassurance and for the first time, I don't want to push someone away.

"My uncle is in town for a bit. I think he said something about watching some game at the sports bar. Do you want to come over for a drink or something?"

There's no way in hell I'd say no to that and we're on the road as soon as I can get the Jeep into gear. I'll admit, I take the roads a little too fast, wanting to get back to her place as soon as possible. Already, I'm thinking about getting my mouth on her. I want to hear her panting for me like I need my next breath. The way she shifts and fidgets in the seat next to me tells me she's in just as much of a rush.

I take the first curve back into town going nearly sixty-five. Peyton leans into my side and I realize I need to calm it down before I get us both into trouble and forgo any chance at getting her naked again. I tap the brakes, but the Jeep doesn't respond. As we pick up speed my hands grow damp on the wheel.

"Ford?" Peyton asks, a slight edge to her voice. "What's wrong?"

The moment the Jeep begins to spin out of control underneath my grip as we take another curve throttling up to seventy-five, adrenaline spikes. "Hold on," I tell Peyton beside me. *Just hold on.*

From the corner of my eye, I see Peyton grip the handles on the dash and above her head. Her face has gone sheet white. I get a flash of despair. I can't let anything happen to her. Not yet. It's too soon.

I don't want to lose anyone else.

The echo of another voice, another life, rings around me. I remember telling Ryan Kent something similar the night we were attacked and my whole world changed. As the Jeep gains speed as we careen down the mountain, I'm overwhelmed by the same stifling dread.

Thinking quickly, I try to recall the upcoming bends in the road. There are a couple more before the road levels out and spits out into a long highway that leads into town. If we can make it through the curves without losing control and without accelerating to dangerous speeds, we might make it.

We have to.

I WANT to ask more questions, but my heart is in my throat and I'm afraid if I open my mouth I'm going to embarrass myself by vomiting all over my lap. All I can do is hold on for dear life like Ford instructed and hope.

"I'm going to downshift once we get around the last curve to cut our speed." Unlike me, Ford is cool under pressure. His eyes are focused on the road, the vehicle, and sometimes on me with a palpable intensity. "Is your seatbelt secure?"

"It's as good as it's gonna get. What can I do?" I wasn't sure I could do anything, but I hated to be helpless.

"Ever driven a stick?"

Hysterical laughter threatens to bubble up. I tamp it down, swallowing hard. "Not since I was sixteen."

"That'll have to work. When I tell you, I want you to put her into third."

I grip the gearshift with sweat-slicked hands. "Ford?"

"Yeah, sunshine?" He navigates around a curve, barely managing to keep the Jeep on four wheels.

"I have to tell you when my dad tried to teach me to drive a stick, I wrecked the transmission."

He barks out a laugh, manages to grin at me. "In this instance, that could be a good thing. Now!"

I slam the gear into what I hope is third and the Jeep lurches violently along with my stomach. Our speed drops, but only by a fraction. We round another curve.

"Second when I say," Ford instructs. He waits until a we have a long length of uninterrupted road. "Now!"

The Jeep jolts again, this time with a whine of protest. Ford tries pumping the brakes, but to no avail. "First, now!"

We slow to a more manageable speed and I release the gearshift with numb hands. I hadn't realized I'd been holding onto it so tight. "What now?" I ask.

"We're gonna pull the e-brake and hope to hell it does it's job."

"But we're slowing down. Once we coast to a stop we should be fine."

Then I see the intersection. I'd forgotten about it. The road we're on cuts East to West and intersects with another going North to South. As luck would have it, as we speed into view, the interaction is packed with cars full of people.

My heart plummets. "Oh, God," I whisper.

Ford reaches across to tug on my seatbelt. I grip the armrest and the center console knowing it won't do any good if we collide with one of the cars, but needing something to hold onto nevertheless. I think of the outing Ford had described with him relaxing in a hammock while I paint. As we hurtle down the road, I cling to the future with that day in it.

With one hand on the steering wheel in a vice-like grip and the other on the e-brake, Ford rounds a final curve and jerks the e-brake up with enough force that the car jerks, then shudders. I'm thrown forward, hard, against the resistance of the seatbelt, hard enough to bruise.

Tires squeal. Someone screams. And time stops.

The engine shrieks and then I'm thrown back against the seat. We rock to a near halt a short distance from the intersections and only a couple yards from the nearest car. Ford angles the Jeep to the side of the road until to comes to a complete stop.

He's out of the door and around to my side before I even have a chance to unbuckle my seatbelt. Ford scoops me from the car and wraps me up into his arms. I cling to him, my fingers knotting into his shirt.

"Are you okay? Are you hurt?"

Unable to speak around the fear lodged in my throat, I press my face into his chest until it clears. "My shoulder, I think the seatbelt gave me a wicked bruise. But I'm fine. God, Ford, you were amazing. We'd be—"

"Don't. Don't you say it." He steps back to look me over, runs his hands over my body in the removed, clinical way I imagined he did if he was in the field when he was a Marine with an injured friend. "You're alright. Christ."

This time, it's me who soothes him. "I'm fine. Absolutely fine." I wrap my arms around his waist and hold on, just like he'd said.

We stay that way until the police officers arrive.

"At least Hadley didn't look at me like I was crazy this time," I comment as we pull into my driveway.

"He better fucking not. Not after today. I'm going to go back into town and put some pressure on him once I've got you settled. You should also report what happened with your clothes."

Uncle Brad looks up as we walk in the door. Noting the look on my face, he quickly gets to his feet and crosses to us. "Peyton. Something happened. What's wrong? Are you okay?"

I hold up a hand. "I'm fine, I'm fine. We just had a little

car trouble. Everything is okay. Ford, this is my Uncle Brad, Uncle Brad, this is Ford."

Ford gives a nod, but I can tell he's not really in the mood for pleasantries. "Sir. If you don't mind, I'd like to get Peyton into bed. She got a little banged up." Without waiting for an answer he leads me through the open door of my bedroom.

"What kind of car trouble leaves you a little banged up?" Uncle Brad demands. He hovers over the bed as Ford urges me under the sheets.

"The kind where my brakes went out and we had to make an emergency pit stop. Got any ice?" Ford asks.

Uncle Brad gapes for a moment, then noticing my wince of pain, hurries to the kitchen.

"Be easy on him," I tell Ford, who tucks me into the blankets like a child. "He's been through a lot and he worries."

"He's not the only one."

"Do you really think I should report what happened with the clothes? It could have been me being forgetful. Besides, we don't know for sure that the two are related."

The look he sends me makes me roll my eyes.

"We're not going to take any chances and I don't want you staying here alone. Do you or your uncle own a gun?"

It would be useless to argue. "No, we don't."

"Then I'm staying here for the night."

"You don't have to do that."

"If you think I'm leaving you alone after what happened today, then you're sorely mistaken."

Uncle Brad comes rushing back. He hands me the pack of ice and I press it against my bruise with a wince. "Thank you."

"I think you should come home with me," Uncle Brad says as he sits on the bedside opposite Ford. "Clearly there is something going on here and I'd like you to come home with me where I can keep an eye on you."

I glare at the both of them. "Are you two conspiring against me? I'm not running away. Uncle Brad, I appreciate your concern, but you have to let me take care of myself at some point. I'm not a child anymore and you can't protect me from everything."

"Tell him," Ford orders.

"Tell me what?"

I wonder if I can lure Ford back to those pretty cliffs and throw him bodily over the edge. I take my uncles hands in mine. "That murder I told you about? We think the person responsible has been trying to hurt me."

"Oh, peanut."

"The sheriff's department has it under control. They're coming back by tomorrow to interview me again."

"I guess it's a good thing I came," he says. It's basically

an I-told-you-so, but considering what just happened, I let it slide.

"I didn't want you to worry and it was something I needed to see through to the finish."

"Are you sure you won't reconsider coming home?" he asks.

I shake my head. "No, I don't want to run away anymore. Besides, I like it here. I don't want to leave yet."

"Then, I'm staying, too. It's too late to check in to a place since your young man is staying with you, but I'm not going to leave until I know your safe."

Ford is practically vibrating with tension next to me, even though he's been respectfully silent. Knowing I'm better off accepting Uncle Brad's decision than arguing, I acquiesce. "I guess I can't argue with you there. Can you give us a minute?" At his pause and, I put steel into my voice and backbone. "Just for a few minutes."

As soon as Uncle Brad's through the door, Ford wraps his arms around me. I sit up so I feel less like an invalid.

"I'm fine," I say preemptively, but he's already running his hands over my face and down my arms again. I wince a little when his fingers tickle over my bruised shoulder. At his frown, I repeat, "I'm fine."

"You're not fine," he replies through gritted teeth. "This is exactly what I was afraid of happening."

His eyes cloud over and he winces as though he's in pain. "When I realized the brakes were out I—" When the words stick in his throat, I scoot over on the bed and offer him a place to sit. "When they went out, I thought I'd already lost you."

I pull him close and touch our foreheads together. It causes my shoulder to twinge painfully, but his touch is like a balm that quiets everything else.

"You didn't lose me," I say into the material of his t-shirt. "I'm right here. I'm right here."

His arms tighten around me, not enough to hurt me, but enough that it reminds him I'm not going anywhere, that I'm safe.

At least for now.

I WAKE UP WITH FORD ALREADY ABOVE ME, HIS WEIGHT a welcome feeling as he pins me to the bed. His mouth cruises down my neck, across my bruised shoulder, and then, finally, to my nipples where he takes his time licking and sucking until I begin to thrash underneath him. He must have pushed my shirt up in the night. I clutch his head to my breast and bite my lip. Knowing we're not alone in the house, I try to keep quiet, but he was right. I'm never quiet.

He lifts his head and I groan in an agony of want. "You

better be quiet, Peyton. Your uncle might hear us and then what would you do?"

"Please, I need you." And I did. I needed that connection to him now more than ever. He said he was afraid something had happened to me, but I shared the same fear. That's all I could think about when we were racing down the road with death as the only outcome: that I wanted to live, wanted the possibility of a future with him.

"I've got you," he says and surges up to take my lips with his.

I sigh in gratitude, knowing I could kiss him forever and my only issue would be wanting more. The bed creaks softly as we struggle out of our clothes. I only manage to get my panties off before his hips are between my legs. Reaching down, I take him in my hand and smile when he inhales sharply against my mouth.

Gripping him tight, I rub the head of his cock against my entrance which causes him to wrap his arms more tightly around me and his kisses turn almost bruising. When it becomes to much, he brushes my hands away and thrusts inside me. I arch my neck and he covers my mouth with a hand to control the resulting moan. He turns my head to the side so he can whisper in my ear.

"You feel so fucking good, little girl. I know you want to scream, but you better be quiet." When he hears my stran-gled cries, he only keeps going. "I'm gonna need you like this every night. Waking up in the middle of the night to find you next to me. I want to fall asleep inside you like this and wake up with you coming around me."

I bite the thick part of his hand and he groans. We both turn to the door when we hear the wood floors creak, but we don't stop. I'm not sure if we could.

"I want to feel you come around me, sunshine. I need it." His teeth nip at my ear. "I thought I lost you today and I need to feel you now more than anything."

His dirty talk switches to sweet nothings and his rhythm slows. It's almost like worship the way he glides in and out of me, the steady stream of endearments intermixed with filthy observations. Just when I think I've got what he's going to say figured out he switches it up and I stumble mentally and emotionally to keep up. He undoes me. It's just that simple.

"God, you look fuckin' beautiful right now. I could look at you forever. Come on that cock, baby. I want to see your face when you do."

Then he leverages up so he can watch my face and my legs wrap tight around his. If I was at the edge, he takes me right over as he tangles my feet with his so they're immobile and then drives so deep inside me I can feel him in places I didn't even know existed.

He covers my mouth with his hand again as I explode around him with stars filling my vision and my ears ringing.

His harsh exhalations puff against my shoulder as he comes along with me.

Later, when we fall asleep, I do so with one leg wrap around his waist with him still inside me. When he wakes me a couple hours later, I'm already halfway to orgasm and this time he doesn't need to speak because there's no need for words.

THE NEXT MORNING, Hadley confirms what I already knew to be true. "Your brake lines were cut. It's a miracle the two of you survived."

I'd been prepared for the news. I hadn't slept a wink next to Peyton all night, my mind racing with scenario after scenario. You couldn't live life as I had and not be prepared for any eventuality. She'd slept peacefully next to me, only rousing long enough for me to make love to her, then falling asleep again. I'd memorized her face as she dreamed and wondered if I'd have to watch her die, too. "Tell me you believe her now. The person who has been in her house moving things around is the same one who tried to kill us yesterday and the one she saw on the lake."

"All I can go by is the evidence I've got in front of me.

According to the tech's yes, someone did cut your lines. Is there anyone who has a grudge against you? Anyone who'd want to hurt you?"

"Plenty of people, c'mon Hadley you're not new in town. You know I'm not Mr. Popular around here."

Hadley frowns. "Anyone here recently?"

"The only person who I've had confrontations with recently are some dude my sister was seeing a couple weeks back. We had a little dust up when he put his hands on her. And Lola. She was upset I wouldn't kick out other guests for her to host her meeting."

"Lola's out of town right now on a conference, but I'll give her a call. Do you know the name of the guy you tussled with?"

I think back, but it doesn't come to me right away. "Not that I can recall, but I can get ahold of my sister and get it from her and get back to you."

"About these clothes we were talking about earlier," he begins, turning to Peyton, who'd been sitting on the porch rocker drinking a cup of coffee. "You said you came home and they were wet again?"

She nods, pushing the rocker with one foot on the porch and the other tucked up underneath her. She's wearing a pair of jeans and a light sweater. Her hair is still damp and her cheeks are vaguely pink from the shower where I'd fucked her against the wall. She meets my eyes before she answers and I have to lock my knees to keep from staggering backward. She's steady. Steady like I haven't seen her since she got here. Her world's been knocked off its axis, but this time, she's not running. I think I fall a little bit in love at her warrior attitude.

She squares her shoulders and looks Hadley directly in the eye. "That's right. The door, I can't remember if it was locked or not when I left home. I was dead tired after a long day at work and my mind is fuzzy about that. I normally triple check because of what happened to my parents. But it was open when I got back. I looked through the whole house, but no one was there. The only thing disturbed were my clothes."

"Why didn't you report the break in the day it happened?" he asked.

"C'mon, Hadley," I interrupt. "She was scared. You didn't exactly lay out the welcome mat the first time, making her think she was seeing things. Jesus Christ."

"It's okay. It's a valid question." She lifts a shoulder and takes another sip of coffee. "At the time I wasn't sure it *wasn't* me being forgetful. You're not wrong to assume that I've had a troubled past and that I was mentally and emotionally unstable for a while after my parents deaths, but that doesn't mean I'm wrong about this. I'm as sane as either of you. I know what I saw that night and I know someone is trying to spook me or worse because of it. Now what are you going to do about it?"

"I HAVE TO SAY, THAT SPINE OF YOURS IS A HELL OF A turn on," I say to Peyton as I drive her into town to drop her off for work.

"There has to be something I'm missing. Something I saw that night that someone thinks will lead me to them. I wish I knew what it was so this could be over. You may think I'm being strong, but it doesn't feel that way."

I glance over at her in the passenger seat. Since my Jeep would be out of commission for the foreseeable future, she's letting me borrow her snazzy little car to get back to the lodge and check on Lexie. "It could be. Even if you didn't when they learned there was a witness, they wouldn't want to risk it. Are you sure you don't want to call in and stay with me at the lodge for the next couple days? I'm sure Alice would understand."

"I would, but I need to keep busy now more than ever or I really will go crazy."

"You'll call me if anything happens. I'll keep my phone on me. If I don't answer, you call Brad or the sheriff. Even if you don't think it's a big deal. I don't want you to take any chances."

Her smile lights up my morning. "I promise I won't." She starts to get out of the car, then stops and leans in to give me a kiss. When she's done and begins to pull away, I tangle my hands in her hair and kiss her longer.

"Let me know when you get off and I'll come pick you up."

"I can have Uncle Brad drive me back," she offers.

"I know you can, but I'll feel better if I come and pick you up."

She rolls her eyes, but she says, "Okay, if you insist. If Hadley gives you any updates—"

"I'll let you know as soon as I hear anything. Take it easy today."

"I will." She pauses for a second, her eyes meeting mine, then darting away. Waving a little, she backs up, then turns and disappears inside the store.

I pull into the lodge a quarter of an hour later and find Lexie and Nell huddled together behind the front counter. They both giggle when they see me walk through the front door.

"What?" I ask.

"Someone got lucky," Lexie comments with a mile-wide grin.

"Alexus Collier," I admonish as I push around the counter. "I don't ever want to hear you say that again."

"Your uncle's right, Lexie. His love life is his own

business." Nell's eyes are dancing when she turns to face me, then grows more serious. "Martha Winfrey, who lives out in the cabin by Alice's said the sheriff was over visiting this morning. Did you guys run into some more trouble?"

Before I can answer, the doors burst open again and Mercy saunters through like she didn't abandon her daughter. "I'm back!" she announces.

The smile slides off Lexie's face and she crosses her arms over her chest.

I straighten and step in front of her, turning to Mercy. "Where the hell have you been?"

She rolls her eyes. "Don't get all bent out of shape. I was only gone for a couple of days and it's not like she's a baby. She can practically take care of herself by now anyways." Mercy shakes out her hair with one manicured claw and then tosses it over her shoulders.

"An uncle who she barely knows in a strange town. You can't just disappear like that without any notice. She's your kid for christ's sake. You can't assume people will always be around to clean up your messes, Mercy. We have lives, too. I've got a business to run and a lot of shit to do that can't just be set to the side for your whims."

"I don't have to listen to this. I've had a long drive and I don't appreciate your tone. Come on, Lexie. I want you to see what pretty presents I've brought back for you." Mercy skirts around me and beelines for Lexie, who steps out of her reach.

"No, I don't want to go anywhere with you. You disappeared and didn't even call me to let me know when you'd be back. I hate you!" She screams, tears running down her cheeks. Mercy takes another tentative step forward, but Lexie spins on her heels and darts down the hallway to my apartment.

"Now look what you've done," Mercy says and then follows after her daughter.

I scrub a hand over my face and wonder if I should be the one calling into work today. There should be sick days for family obligations, especially when it came to the female species.

"Give them some time," Nell advises and pats my arm. When the phone rings, she picks it up, her greeting cheerful. "Bear Lake Lodge, Nell speaking."

She extends her arm. "It's for you. It's Sheriff Hadley."

I lean a hip against the counter. "Hadley. Now really isn't a good time, can I call you back later?"

His sigh fills a line. "'Fraid not. I sent a couple deputies down to the lot where you said you were yesterday. While they were there some civilians flagged them down. Jesus, Ford. They found the body. She'd been dumped in the ravine down below Windy Point. A couple of daytrippers stumbled across her."

"She?" I can't seem to breathe. It's irrational, but I imagine Peyton lifeless, skin pale as death, and eyes dull and staring into nothingness and it rocks me to the core.

"Christ, Ford. It's Lola. She's dead. I'm gonna need you to come in and talk."

CHAPTER TWENTY ONE
PEYTON

"Should I come now?" I ask when I call Ford back after seeing his text at my first break. "I can catch a cab or I can ask Alice to bring me over."

"No, you should stay there. I have to go talk to Hadley at the station first. I'll have Nell bring your car to you if you wouldn't mind dropping her back off at her house."

I want to ask him if he's sure. More than that, I want to be there because I don't like the vacant tone in his voice. "That's fine if you're sure. God, I can't believe it was Lola. Her restaurant was the first place I stopped when I got into town."

"I have to go," he says abruptly. "Don't leave the studio without someone there."

"I won't."

Then the line goes dead.

Dread pools in my stomach. I turn to go into the studio and find Alice locking up, her face snow-white and lips bloodless.

"I'm sorry, Peyton, but we have to close today. My sister —" her voice cuts out and tears spill over her cheeks. She dashes them away with her hands. "I just got the call she was found dead. She was supposed to be gone for a conference. I figured that's why I hadn't heard from her, but...The police just found her. I have to go. I'll let you know when we plan to reopen."

She doesn't give me a moment to offer comfort or share sympathy. For the first time since I began working with her, granted not a long time, she looks harried and distracted. With an attention for detail that could rival Nell's, Alice is usually so put together it makes me envious. Understandably, not today.

I blow out a breath and dig my phone back out of my pocket. Ford is going to be at the Sheriff's station for a while. I should spend time with Uncle Brad before he goes home—or at least spend time convincing him he *should* go home. It'll be a hard sell considering the news, but I don't need a babysitter no matter what either of them think.

"I'm glad you called me," Uncle Brad says as we take a seat for lunch at the local Mexican joint.

I order a sangria and extra queso from the waitress and he gets a coke. "Thanks for coming out to lunch with me. I figure we both have some things to talk about."

His salt-and-pepper beard twitches. "Oh? And what did you want to talk about?"

"In case you haven't heard, the police have found the body of a woman this morning. If I'm right it's going to turn out to be the woman I saw killed at the lake." Before he can interrupt me, I raise my hand and cut him off. "No, I'm not coming home. I don't want to keep running away or hiding when things get rough."

The waitress delivers our drinks and Uncle Brad takes a careful sip of his before he answers. "You're being unreasonable. I just want you to be safe."

I nod. "And I will be, right here."

"You can't claim it's safe here when you've got a murderer in your bed."

"What are you talking about?" Derailed, I place my queso covered chip on my plate. Rage causes my hands to tremble, so I hide them under the table on my lap.

"I've read up on your man. Seems he got into some trouble overseas during his last deployment."

"I've heard about that, his niece told me."

"But did *he* tell you? Have you looked it up for yourself?"

My appetite evaporates. "What are you saying?"

He begins to speak and immediately I want him to stop. "He killed a teammate, Peyton. Cold-blooded murder. They were attacked and his teammate was holding them back. He stole morphine from the team medic and injected enough into the wounded Marine to kill a horse. That's why he was discharged. Of course, they couldn't prove it, so it wasn't dishonorable, but the media and the courts had a field day for a couple years."

"You're mistaken." My voice trembles and Uncle Brad reaches across to squeeze my shoulder.

"I'm not. This morning when I got to my room, I did some research. I know you think it's ridiculous, but I wasn't comfortable with you seeing someone when you're clearly so vulnerable."

"I'm not vulnerable," I say slowly, clearly.

"You may think you're not, but you don't even know the person it is that you're seeing. I don't want you to get hurt again."

I study the wood grain in the varnished table, my stomach rolling from the scents of cilantro and salt which had been so appetizing only a few minutes prior. When I'm steady again, I meet my uncle's gaze.

"I came here to ask you to go home, but now I'm telling you. Go home. Whether or not I'm making a mistake is my business. You don't know Ford, and whatever happened to him in his past is his to decide how to tell me. Drive safe," I tell him, then toss a five on the table. "This should pay for the drinks."

I walk out on legs as steady as jelly, my world shaken, exactly as Uncle Brad had intended. Except he figured I'd be the same frightened girl who had hidden when her parents were murdered. I'm not going to hide, I'm not going to run. Not even from the secrets Ford is keeping.

Thirty minutes later, I climb up the steps to my rental, a cold sweat prickling over my skin. I should have called a cab, should have asked Nell for a ride, but I wanted to be alone with my thoughts, needed the fresh, crisp air to clear my head. I'm tired of letting everyone else dictate my life.

I plan to call Ford, maybe work on some art, but first I need the restroom. I'm just finishing up my business when I hear a door jiggle and then open. I can't tell if it's the front or the back and I don't know which is worse.

I pause with my pants still somewhere around my ankles. At first I figure the trepidation that curses around the back of my neck is embarrassment and the responding vulnerability at being caught using the bathroom, but the alarm is all too swift and familiar.

There's someone else in the house.

All I can think is *no, not again.*

Adrenaline spurts through my body and everything speeds up and slows down at the same time. I freeze in the action of pulling my pants up, afraid to make any sound for fear that whoever just came inside will realize I'm here. At first I think it could be Nell checking on me at Ford's request, but the lengthy pauses between footsteps indicate the person inside is being careful not to draw any attention to themselves.

They don't want to be caught.

If it was someone I knew, they would have let me know they were coming. Or they would have knocked. I almost have a hard time trusting my own instincts. It wouldn't be the first time that I imagined something along these lines. Someone in the house, stalking me, waiting for me. Things misplaced, scents in the air that weren't there. It was enough to drive a girl crazy.

Maybe I am. Sometimes it feels like it.

Focus.

As the footsteps grow closer I wrap my arms around myself to stem the shaking that threatens to overtake me. Then I remember there's no car in the drive. Whoever it was would have left when they realized there was no-one home.

Either way, I'm stuck in a house with a person who shouldn't be here. Or confined with my own demons.

I'm not sure which is worse.

Their footsteps stop at the bathroom door and tears slip down my cheeks and spill onto my naked lap. If they chance opening the door, I'm screwed. I glance around, but there's nothing in my immediate vicinity that I can use to defend myself. Even worse, my legs are starting to go numb from sitting for too long. The helplessness is paralyzing. And here I'd thought I'd be able to confront the monsters in the dark if I ever came face to face with one again.

But I'm anything but brave like I'd insisted to Uncle Brad.

In fact, instead of staying to fight, my first response is to flee. The window to my left is too small for me to wiggle my way through, but I latch onto it anyway. Carefully, as I hear the footsteps move on from outside the bathroom to other parts of the living area, I get back to my feet and finish pulling up my pants and zipping them as quietly as possible. I give a passing thought to locking the bathroom door, but I'm afraid even that small sound will give me away.

The bathroom window is maybe ten inches across, if that. Even if it wasn't painted shut and I could fit through it, there's a fence just underneath that bisects the yard between my house and the one next to it. Sweat pops out on my skin, my hands grow damp, and my heart races more as the feeling of the walls closing in around me increases.

I know this only ends one of a couple ways. The person will find what they're looking for and leave, which is the least likely, they'll get spooked and light out at the first sound, or they'll find me in their search and do God only knows what to me.

As I think it, their footsteps recede away and I let out a long, silent breath. Maybe today is my lucky day. I could be wrong and it's just Nell or my uncle coming to check on me and it's my overactive imagination running wild again. I almost open the door to call out to them, until I hear the footsteps heading toward the back of the house, which isn't visible to the bathroom door.

I decide I'll make a dash for the living room where I left my phone. I'll grab it and then haul ass to the front door and call the police as soon as I'm out in the street around people. No one thinks they'll get robbed or have their house broken into in the middle of the day. There's something about the reassuring presence of sunlight that belies the danger, but that's what makes it all the more terrifying.

I whip around the corner, my eyes on the hallway leading to the backdoor, but no one's there. Three careful steps, then I'm in the living room. My phone is a couple feet away and that's where I should be going. And I take a step in the direction of sensibility—to the coffee table where my phone lies in wait—and contemplate my next move.

This isn't going to happen to me again. I won't let it. I complete the distance, dialing 9-1-1 before I can second guess myself. I know what I heard. There's someone in the house who shouldn't be there. They answer on the second ring.

I don't give them time to ask the questions I know are coming. I give my address. "There's an intruder in the house. I'm alone." Then I hang up the phone and continue to the stairs. They said a cruiser was five minutes away, but that could be five minutes too late.

Three years ago, I waited...and it cost me everything.

My therapist would say my reckless behavior is self-destructive. My therapist is an idiot, I decide, and tiptoe to the kitchen.

Whoever was in the house could be the person who tampered with our brakes. I can't let them get away without at least trying to determine who it is—and what they want.

I'm two steps from the kitchen when I hear it. A loud, unmistakable thump, but in the direction of my room. I twist and leap in one bound and land hard in the hallway, skidding into the wall opposite with a crash. I pause, trying to discern their response, but all I hear is my own heartbeat. They must know they aren't alone now.

I put my back to the bathroom and consider the two closed doors, the possibilities. The spare room or mine. I choose the spare, but no one is there, then sprint for my bedroom. I swing open the door, heart galloping in my chest.

And find another empty room.

The side window had been smashed out—that must have been the crash I heard. Broken glass litters the floor and a chilly breeze washes over my face, drawing my attention to the cold sweat clinging to my brow. I double check the closet, under the bed, behind the door, but it's pointless.

Whoever was here is long gone.

The police arrive and take a report, drawing the attention of my neighbors. By the time they leave, I feel more of a fool than I have in a long, long time. Probably just some kids messing around, they said. Or maybe my boyfriend is tangled up with some nasty people and I should ditch him.

Despite the body they'd found, they didn't believe me.

I know what I heard. What I saw. What I felt. Those things had to be real.

Didn't they? Or am I just chasing ghosts.

CHAPTER TWENTY TWO
FORD

"When was the last time you saw the victim?"

"What were you doing at seven p.m. the night of the 23rd?"

"Did you and the victim have a personal relationship?"

The questions begin to blur together after the second hour into the interrogation comes and goes. A stale cup of coffee sits at my elbow, untouched. Hadley and another officer share a look across from me.

I'd been in a room just like this after they picked us up from the desert. Covered in blood, I'd been shuffled off to another room for a debrief. I didn't mind. There was nothing they could do or say to make me feel worse than I already did. It was a numb sort of pain. The kind that blotted out everything else. If I'd been in my right mind, I would have been concerned about the consequences.

But at the time I figured fuck the consequences.

"Tell us what happened," they'd said. "From the beginning."

Step by step, I'd recounted the night as best I could. I stumbled over the recollection of Tate's death. My throat closed on the words, but I didn't hold anything back.

"After the explosion, I found the medic from the Marine support unit. It was chaos and he was busy helping others with injuries. Those who had a chance of survival. It wasn't his fault. While he was distracted, I got in his pack, took the meds. Tate and I had made a pact about what would happen in this situation."

It had been more Tate's idea than mine. He was a good man, a great leader, but a proud one. He never wanted to go home broken, unable to live a normal life. Tate was strong in many ways, but that wasn't one of them. He wasn't like Scott, couldn't fathom the thought of being less than the warrior he'd been his whole life.

"I held him as the life bled out of him. If you want to say I killed him, then that's fair. I'll take whatever punishment is coming to me. I'm sure there's documentation of his wishes. Call me a killer, call me a traitor. I did what I thought I had to do for a friend who had no other options."

They'd grilled me long into the night and into the next day. I could barely walk by the time they cordoned me off in a cell. By then, I was just grateful for a place to shower and sleep.

"Ford," Hadley says sharply, drawing me back from the memories and the scent of blood and dirt.

"What?" I ask.

"I said you can go, but stay close. We may have more questions."

I nod, head swimming from past to present and back again until I can barely tell the difference.

When I get to my feet, Hadley puts a hand to my arm, stopping me as the other detective leaves us alone in the room.

"I thought we were done."

"Look, while this investigation is ongoing, I have to do my job."

I don't fight him. "I get it. It's not your fault. I want you to find out what happened." The sooner he did, the sooner everything could go back to normal. "I have to get back to the lodge, check on my family." And Peyton, but I didn't say it out loud. Now that Lola had been found and her story had been validated, it was no longer an option that she stay in town. It wasn't safe. Hell, the night Tate had been killed we'd been surrounded by some of the most elite military in the world and he still hadn't been safe.

They'd already tried to take her life once. I won't let them get a second chance. I'd make sure of it.

"Before you go, there's something else."

"Spit it out," I growl. I didn't have time for this shit.

"Peyton. She reported a break in this afternoon at her place. I sent some deputies out to take her statement. She's alright, now Ford, but she's understandably shaken up."

"I gotta go," I say over my shoulder as I push through the door. It slaps against the wall and crashes shut. I can feel Hadley's eyes on me as I cut through the crowded onlookers.

Mercy calls. I answer with a terse, "Not right now."

"There's reporters camped out on the front lawn. You want me to get out the .22?"

"Only if they start hassling you. Call Hadley if they give you any problems. Offer the guests free food and booze to compensate for the inconvenience. I've gotta go check on Peyton, her house was just broken into." Silence answers me. "Did you hear me?" Now is not the time for Mercy's shit. "Do I need to call Nell instead?"

"I'm not an idiot. I'll handle things here."

"Don't fuck it up, Mercy," I say, then end the call.

I'd pay for the comment later, but I didn't care. I come around the curve to Peyton's place seconds later, tires screaming and spitting gravel. She meets me on the porch, her arms wrapped around her waist. Her gaze pins me to the seat of her tiny ass car the way it cuts through me. The soft sweater she's wearing bares one of her shoulders. Her golden-blonde hair tumbles down her back.

I want nothing more than to charge right up to her and take her into my arms, console her. Make it all better. I need to feel her against me, but because I need it so much, want it so much, I force myself to take measured steps across the small yard and up the steps.

"Are you hurt?" I ask first, surprised that it wasn't the first thing I'd asked Hadley when he told me.

Her gaze is shuttered closed. Impenetrable. She's not locked inside her house this time, but that doesn't mean she's letting me inside her head or heart right now, either. Guess I wasn't the only one dealing with the fallout. Or not dealing with it.

"Are you hurt?" I repeat.

She shakes her head. "I'm fine."

Woman-speak for you should know I'm not fine.

"Let's go inside."

She doesn't move. "I'm fine out here."

"What happened?"

"Alice shut down the store today. Lola was her sister, you know? So I had lunch with Uncle Brad. We argued. I walked home to cool off."

"Alone?" I cut in.

She ignores me. "A little while after I got home, someone came in. Started looking around. I want to say it was just someone looking for easy cash, but I don't know anymore. The cops didn't seem to take it seriously."

"They should have."

Her shoulder lifts, dismissing me. "It doesn't matter. They've found the woman and that's all that matters. Are you okay?"

"I'm alright. What did you and your Uncle argue about?"

"He thinks it's too dangerous here. That I should go home."

The opening is easy, so I take it. Better to get it over with than drag it out. "Maybe your Uncle was right."

Her eyes widen. She wasn't expecting me to agree with him. No doubt she was prepared to have me beg to keep her, ask her to stay, or maybe not. But I'd rather be damned to hell than put her in danger.

"What do you mean? I thought you said everything was going to be okay." Her words are as dull as her eyes and it cuts me deep to know I'm the reason for it after seeing them filled with such life.

I pace the porch, knowing if I don't get the words out I won't ever be able to say them. "That was before you nearly got yourself killed. It's not safe for you here and if you weren't being so damn stubborn you'd be able to see that."

Her back goes up and she clenches her fists by her sides. I can see the anger light her eyes and wish I wasn't so damn stubborn myself. If I were any closer, I'd be worried she'd put that right hook to good use.

"I'm never safe anywhere," she says, throwing her hands up in the air. "That's what the two of you don't seem to understand. I can't live my life like I'm going to die. I can't always play it safe."

"I don't give a damn about what I don't understand. I thought I could keep you protected, but if the last twenty-four hours haven't proven the opposite, then I don't know what to tell you." A million different scenarios race through my thoughts and all of them end with me finding *her* covered in blood.

"It's not your job to be my protector. I'm with you because I want to be." She swallows audibly and my chest goes tight. "What are you trying to say here, Ford? That you're scared because something might happen to me? Or that you're scared because something is happening *with* me."

I turn my back to her and press my palms into the deck. She sounds so hurt and it makes me sick to my stomach. But I'll do whatever it takes, even if it means breaking her heart. "If that's what you want to believe, then fine. But you know I'm right. It's insane for you to stay here."

Her steps follow me to the railing. Her touch is hesitant at first as she reaches me, the tips of her fingers tracing along my bunched shoulders and down my arm to grab the hand I didn't know was digging into the countertop. I should push her away, but I can't make myself do it.

"Nothing happened to me. I'm fine."

When I don't answer, she presses against my shoulder and I relent, turning to face her. She pauses before taking the final step to bring her body fully against mine.

I release a breath I didn't know I was holding, one that feels like it's been pent up since I nearly lost her the day before.

I kiss her once, softly, then take a step back. "I can't do this. I have to go."

"Ford," she calls out behind me. "Ford, wait!"

I don't take her car in case she needs it, so I walk the couple miles back to the lodge.

She doesn't follow me.

Covered in sweat, I push in the front door, my anger simmering just beneath the surface. The reporters swarming the front yard are a furious buzz of noise and movement behind me.

"Uncle Ford," Lexie shouts. "I thought you'd gone to jail."

Mercy comes out from behind the counter as Lexie throws herself into my arms. "Are you okay?" she mouths over Lexie's head.

"I'm fine," I say to both of them.

"You don't look fine," Lexie says. "You look sad."

Trust a kid to get straight to the heart of it. "I promise I'm alright, sweetheart. There's a lot going on right now. Why don't you go help Nell sort out the late night crowd, okay?"

She pauses, but I give her a little nudge and she says, "Don't go to bed without me, I have to tell you what happened with Cody!"

Lexie scampers off with Nell, who gives me a pointed glance. I turn back to Mercy. She arches a brow at me.

"What?"

"Nothing, not a thing," she says with a smirk.

"Don't fucking start with me."

"I didn't say a word."

"You've got that look."

Mercy follows as I duck behind the counter for something, anything, to keep me busy and take my mind off everything. "I don't have any look." But there's humor in her voice and it grates on my last nerve.

"You have no idea what's going on, Mercy."

She snorts. "Please, like it's some sort of mystery. I knew once I saw that girl it would only be a matter of time before you kicked her to the curb. You're a serial monogamist, but as soon as it gets too serious you flake out."

"And you're better? Why the fuck are you even here

Mercedes? Why do you keep putting Lexie through this bullshit. You talk about me getting my shit together? At least I don't drag my daughter around the country chasing strange cock. You want to talk shit about my life? Take a look at your own before you cast judgements. You don't know half the shit I went through."

"Don't talk to her like that," Lexie says from behind me. I turn and find her holding plates and silverware, her expression stunned and tears spilling over her cheeks. "You don't get to talk to my momma like that."

Lexie shoves the plates at me, then yanks on her mother's arm and shoots me a look so full of loathing I wonder if maybe her mom taught it to her or if she came by it naturally. She tucks Mercy under her shoulder and hurries her from the room, leaving me alone with my regrets.

CHAPTER TWENTY THREE
PEYTON

I THROW myself in my art so I don't have to think about anything else.

Not the fact that Ford dumped me. Not the fact that it hurts so damn much.

Certainly not why I care about one or the other.

As the days pass, the investigation continues. I tell myself I'm not waiting to hear from Ford, but every time my phone rings with a call or text or I hear a car out on the gravel, I'm disappointed when it's not him.

Alice is busy arranging the funeral and dealing with the police, so there's no telling when she'll open Splatters back up. In the meantime, I've been job hunting hoping she'll give me a break on rent, but not wanting to ask considering the circumstances. I thought I had my life figured out when

I drove into town on a mission. I couldn't have been more wrong.

So in between job hunting and waiting for news about the investigation, I lock myself away in my spare room and bleed onto the canvas.

In art, there are no one's expectations but my own. Well, at least until it's out of my hands. I can create purely to please, amuse, or distract myself. I let it consume me to the point where days pass and I pay no mind. The lamps I set up in the spare room create a casino-like effect where I don't notice the sun rising or falling. All I see is the finished product in my mind's eye and the steps I must take to get there.

I come to, blinking blearily at my surroundings, and realize the stench that's distracting me isn't the noxious smell of paints, it's me. With a grimace, I wash my brushes and store the painting for later, even though my fingers are itching to dive back in. A refreshing shower, some food, and a good glass of wine will help me clear my head of the distractions.

A trail of clothes mark my journey to the the shower and pile on the tile floor at the base of the sink. Arms too sore from the constant back and forth of angry brushstrokes, I just leave the clothes right where they lay to deal with later. The hot spray sluices over my shoulders and I moan in relief. My aching muscles never make themselves known after a long stint in front of the easel until I manage to pull myself from the creative trance and boy are they screaming at me.

The paint isn't the only thing the hot sluicing water washes away. Or at least that's what I tell myself. But no matter how many showers I take, no matter how hard I scrub my skin clean, nothing can take away the throbbing hurt at the center of my chest.

Now that my mind isn't preoccupied with the canvas, it's free to wander. To worry. To obsess.

Purposefully, I uncap the shampoo and focus on spreading the solution over my hair and lathering it into suds. Over the years I've learned I can control my anxiety in one of three ways: art, sex, or routine.

Everything in my life revolves around keeping the memories, and the accompanying stress, at bay. When I can't paint, and when obsessing about the order in which I conduct my life doesn't even help, sex was my go-to.

Until Ford.

Now, I can't think of anything but him and I wonder if sex will ever be the same without those filthy, sweet words in my ear as I go over the edge.

As I carefully spread cream over my legs, I consider that maybe men in general are more trouble than they're worth.

Granted, I don't normally choose men like Ford. My typical type is overworked, slightly younger, and more than happy to satisfy my need for no strings.

Ford, however, didn't fit any of that criteria.

And look where that got me.

"I can't thank you enough for coming in," Alice says, concern knitting her brow. Behind her the parents of today's birthday girl hover with matching nervous expressions.

"It's no problem, Alice." I hadn't expected the call, but I was grateful. Money was already tight and I wanted to do something, anything, to help. "Are you sure you don't want to go home? Be with your husband. I can take care of things here or we can call in Carrie."

After a week of painting and being cooped up, I was starting to get antsy. Alice's husband Jim had come along with her and he sat, hovering on the edges, his face taut with worry. The other manager Carrie had offered, but Alice turned her down. There were three birthday parties back to back today and after the funeral, Alice had called me in to help because she didn't want to cancel on the kids.

"Can we have the canvases now?" the mother asks.

I force a smile. "Of course, let me run and get those."

Alice follows me back to the stockroom and I glance at

her over my shoulder. "Are you sure you don't want to go home?" I repeat. "I know how annoying it is to get asked that all the time, believe me when my parents died, I got enough concern to last a lifetime. I want you to know I'm here if you need anything at all."

Her eyes are red and still swollen. No amount of makeup can cover the dark shadows underneath. The smile she works up trembles a little, and her hands shake when she moves to help me grab supplies for the parties. "Now, Peyton I don't want to get upset with you, but if one more person asks me if I'm sure that I'm okay I may scream. We've got work to do and honestly, being busy will help me more than anything else."

I pile canvases on my arm and extend them to her. "Well then, we'd better get back to work before my boss fires me."

She gives me a thin smile. "We'd better get these to those children before they cause a riot. We'll need twelve of those canvases now. And don't forget the party favors, okay?"

"Right behind you," I tell her as I gather the supplies.

We manage to finish the first two parties and are wrapping up the last without any major incidents. Alice's husband Jim watches from the corner and normally it wouldn't bother me, but there's something about his eyes that makes me feel off-kilter. I keep my distance as I flit back and forth between the supply room and the party rooms.

He snags me on one such trip and pulls me to the side. His breath is rank and I fight to keep from shrinking back. Someone has been hitting the liquor cabinet. I try, and fail, at not judging. "Can I help you with something?" I ask. Maybe if I don't breathe in, I won't have to smell him.

"I heard you were there, the night Lola was killed. Alice and I used to go out on the boat there all the time."

I'd had a few people stop and pump me for details so while this wasn't uncommon, it never failed to make me uncomfortable. "I was, but I have to get back to—"

"If she would have stayed home, this never would have happened. She was always so headstrong. Argumentative. She drove everyone crazy." I don't know if it's the wild look in his eyes or the vice grip he as on my arm, but a cold chill sneaks down my spine.

"I'm sorry?"

But it's almost like he doesn't hear me. "I told her not to go, but she didn't listen. She never listened."

"Jim? Are you okay? Should I get Alice?"

His eyes focus on me for the first time, then clear. He straightens and runs a hand through his hair. "I'm fine. No, don't get her. I think I'll go home and get some rest."

He stumbles out the door and I stand, stunned, and wonder what the hell just happened. My mind races to catch up, but one remark sticks out. He and Alice have a boat. They used to go to Bear Lake all the time.

I grip the shelf next to me, knocking over a ceramic fox someone had painted. It crashes to the ground and all eyes turn to me.

Could Jim have had something to do with the murder? Was he the man I'd seen?

Staggered, I retrieve the broom and dustpan to sweep up the mess before one of the children get hurt. Once I have a spare moment, I sneak off to the break room to tap out a text to Ford.

Call me as soon as you get this.

I don't know if he'll answer, but he's the only person I know to turn to. The sheriff's department made me feel like I was insane. Going to them without any concrete proof feels like a fool's errand.

Ten minutes later, I check my phone again, but there was no read receipt. *Dammit, Ford.* Tears prick the back of my eyes. What am I going to do?

I need to talk to him. Need to hear his voice. I don't care if that makes me needy or demanding, dammit.

"Peyton?" Alice calls over the sound of chattering children. From the high pitched tone of her voice, I can tell her patience with me is wearing as thin as her smile. "Will you get more canvases, please?"

She must not have seen her husband. Understandable,

considering what she's going through. Poor Alice. How the hell am I going to tell her about this?

Mind racing, I tuck my phone back into my pocket. I have to think quickly. Much as I want to say something to Alice, I want to talk it over with Ford first...but if I'm right—and I have to be—we need to come up with a plan to keep her safe. Considering the annoyed looks she sends as soon as I come out with the canvases and tray of art favors, she may not be willing to listen to everything I have to say if I come to her by myself.

"Here we go!" I say with false cheer. "Who's ready to paint?"

As I pass out more favors, little tin trays filled with watercolor paints, my mind is on my phone burning a hole in my pocket. I leave it in on vibrate in case Ford tries to call back, but he doesn't and by the time the party ends an hour later, I'm frantic.

I clean up going double time, making more of a mess in my hurry to finish, but I can't seem to control my hands.

"Alright, now that everyone's gone, you need to tell me what's going on. Now, I've tried not to buy into any of the nonsense going on around town about Ford and your past, but this is business, girl. You've got to keep your head on straight or it affects my bottom line. I can't have that, especially now."

"I'm sorry, Alice. Truly. I hate to put you in the middle

of this and ordinarily, I wouldn't want to cause any trouble. Normally, I wouldn't ask, but I haven't heard from Ford and I'm really worried. Do you mind if I have Carrie come in to cover the rest of the day?"

Alice takes off her glasses, polishes them with a clean end of her apron. "Tell me what's going on and then we'll figure out what to do."

Unable to sit still, I take out a wet wipe and begin washing the kid-sized table of paint splotches, spilled water, and crumbs from leftover cake. "I don't want to bring you into this. You've already done so much for me and you're right, I shouldn't bring personal problems into work. Once I finish here, though, I'll need to go and I understand if you have to let go me for it."

I finish wiping the table and begin stacking the miniature chairs upside down in preparation to mop the floors. As soon as I'm done, I'll drive back to the lodge and hunt Ford down myself. And Lord help him when I do find him. I'm going to personally attach his phone to his body if I have to solder it to his hand myself.

Alice, who'd disappeared once I started mopping, comes back into the room and stops me from resetting the unused supplies from the party. "Let's go," she says and jiggles her keys. "I'll take you to the lodge and we'll track Ford down."

I blink at her, not understanding. "No, you don't have to do that."

"I insist. You look as nervous as a long-tail cat in a room full of rocking chairs. C'mon now. We'll worry about this mess tomorrow." When I could only stare at her, she rolled her eyes and tugged my arm. Unable to protest, I followed her to her big white S.U.V. "Go on, get in there. We'll be over to the lodge in a couple minutes and we'll get this all settled. I have to tell you though, honey, no man is worth worrying yourself over. Especially not one with a temper like that Ford of yours."

"He's doesn't have a temper, he's just...moody."

The engine roars to life and I put on my seatbelt automatically, torn between social convention and guilt. If Jim had killed Lola, and I was pretty sure he did, Alice would be devastated. I hate the thought of watching another family ripped apart like mine had been, but Lola deserved justice, no matter what happened after. If I could have found the person responsible for my parents' deaths, I would have. Now I have a chance to serve up redemption for someone who lost their life violently and I'll see it through, no matter what.

"Thank you for taking me," I say when I've got my voice back.

"Not a problem."

The air from the vents blows out freezing and I shiver,

or maybe it's the nerves. Ford said he was going to be at the lodge all day. There's no reason why he couldn't answer his phone. The thought occurs to me that Nell might know where he is, so I call the lodge as Alice navigates through traffic.

Nell answers with a cheerful trill, "Bear Lake Lodge, this is Nell. How may I help you today?"

If I weren't sitting, my knees would have buckled from the intense relief at her familiar voice. "Nell, thank goodness."

"Peyton, that you? What's wrong? You sound dreadful."

"Nothing. I mean I'm fine. Is Ford there? Can I talk to him?"

There's a pause and for a moment I think she's passing him the phone, followed by static and then, "No, honey, I'm sorry. He went out with Mercy and Lexie for a while. Something the matter?"

My stomach sinks. "Oh, okay. No, everything is fine." My tongue sticks to the roof of my mouth at the lie as it's gone desperately dry with renewed panic. "If you see him before I get there will you have him call me, please?"

"Sure thing, doll. Are you sure everything's okay?"

"Yes. Thanks, Nell," I say and then hang up before her southern hospitality can pull the truth from my lips.

"We're almost there," Alice says. "Now why don't you really tell me what's going on that's got you so frazzled. This got to do with Lola and that stuff Ford told Sheriff Hadley's been going on at his place?"

"I've already caused you enough trouble," I say and bite my tongue. And I'm going to cause so much more.

"You find something out?"

I want to reach over and shove my own foot on the gas. I know everything moves slower in the south and Alice is driving the speed limit, but everything inside me is screaming at her to go faster.

"I'm not sure yet," I edge, trying to keep my voice level.

"C'mon now, Peyton. We're friends aren't we? If it's about Lola, I think I deserve to know."

At the hurt tone in her voice, I relent a little. She's been nothing but kind to me and I'm treating her like she's the criminal instead of Jim. "I think—" I have to clear my throat when my voice breaks. "Jim mentioned the two of you had a boat. That he likes to go fishing."

"Yes, of course. We have a house on the lake. It's a family house but we share it when we can. Why? What's this about?"

"Do you—do you know what he was doing the night she went missing?"

Alice gives me a sidelong glance as she turns down the road leading to the lodge. "Why are you asking me that?"

"When I was talking to him just now, he mentioned trying

to talk Lola out of leaving. That they may have argued. He talked about how the two of you used to go fishing out on the lake all the time." I hate to be the one to tell anyone this sort of news, but she has to know. Panic grips my insides. It didn't occur to me before, but Alice could be in danger from Jim once she knows. "Alice, I think Jim may have had something to do with her death. I'm so sorry to be the one to tell you."

She slams on the brakes and a terrified squawk squeezes from my chest as the safety belt bites into my flesh. Her hand grips my elbow, the long red-painted nails digging in so deep I swear I can feel them drawing blood.

"Why would you say something like that, after all I've done for you?"

I grip her wrist, but she's stronger than she looks. My stomach rolls and my fingers go cold.

"I'm sorry. I'm probably wrong. What do I know?" I babble. Anything to get her to calm down the crazy look she's giving me. We're so close to the lodge. Once I get there and find Ford, I'll be safe. He'll keep me safe. "I don't know what I'm talking about."

For one long, tense moment, Alice's eyes rove over my face and I try to clear my expression. Finally, she takes her foot off the brake and we inch forward. "I'm sure rest is all you need," she says. "Let me get you back to Ford's."

I let my head fall back against the headrest and allow

my eyes to shut for a moment. "Thank you, Alice. I really appreciate it."

"Don't think anything of it," she says.

Ford, please be there.

We hit a huge bump and my stomach jolts. My eyes shoot open and I realize she'd taken the fork that leads away from the lodge. "Alice, you're going the wrong way. The right fork goes to the lodge."

She doesn't answer and I sit straight up in my seat and for a second, I'm back in the basement, stuck in a confined space with the man who killed my parents...except this time there is nowhere to run, nowhere to hide.

"Alice? Did you hear me? You're going the wrong way." I try to modulate my response, but it comes out shaky.

She turns off onto a side road—in the opposite direction of the lodge. My legs flex in anticipation to run, but there's nowhere to go. Breath heaves out of me like I've finished a marathon.

"Alice?"

"Stop talking," she bites out. "Christ, you've got the biggest mouth this side of the Mason-Dixon. I thought keeping you close where I could keep an eye on you would be smart, but Lord if you aren't a pest."

My mouth goes dry and my mind goes blank. "What are you saying?"

She snorts. "You know for someone who thinks they

know everything you're as dumb as a rock. Jim didn't kill Lola, you idiot. I did."

I don't have a moment to fight back because as soon as I look over, she strikes out and my head explodes with darkness.

"ARE you sure you don't want to stay a little while longer? I didn't mean for you to move out."

Mercy looks up from the box she's carrying and wipes sweat from her forehead. "No, you were right. I haven't been doing right by Lexie. She deserves a nice home, a stable life. Just because I had her when I was young doesn't mean she should pay for my mistakes."

"Look at you acting all grown up."

Mercy hip checks me as we drop off our load in the living room of the small rental she'd found the day before. "Watch it, baby brother."

"Hey, Uncle Ford," Lexie says as she bounds in the door carrying her suitcase and a box. "This one has your name on it."

I give Mercy a sidelong glance. "Trying to steal some of my stuff."

She holds up her hands. "I plead the fifth. I'll be right back, I'm gonna grab another load."

Lexie scampers off to her room and I investigate the box. It's a small one from the post office. I vaguely remember seeing it a couple weeks ago before everything went down. It has my name on it.

And Tate.

It's from Tate's mother.

Jesus Christ.

I have to sit on the corner of Mercy's bargain basement couch as I hold the box away from me like it's a live grenade. There's no telling what's inside it. I'm not even sure I want to know.

It can't be anything good.

I'm saved from figuring it out when Mercy comes back in. "Help me with this?" she asks. I set the package by my keys to remember to take home later and grab the top box from her stack.

She puts it down on the kitchen counter and turns to me with a serious look on her face. "I want to apologize," she begins. I start to wave her away, but she catches my wrist. "No, I mean it. I'm sorry. For being such a bitch and not considering how you'd react if I showed up with no warning. I shouldn't have left Lexi with you the way I did. I guess the both of us can be real jerks sometimes."

Pulling her into a hug, I kiss the top of her head. "You were already forgiven, short stuff. But what do you mean both of us?"

She smirks up at me. "Peyton, you jackass. You haven't exactly been fair to her."

I don't know what I'd rather *not* talk or think about more: what's in that package or Peyton. "I don't want to get into this," I say.

"That's the point. We've buried everything for so long it's gotten to be routine to ignore the important shit. You like her. Hell, you may even love her. Don't push her away now like you've done everyone else."

She won't give it up and I haven't talked to or seen Peyton since I left her place the week before. Not knowing if she's okay has been slowly killing me.

"Since we're sharing, the truth is, I think I fucked up. I haven't told her the horrible shit that happened to me. I didn't want the same thing to happen again. I pushed her away so I wouldn't lose her. How fucked up is that?"

Mercy chuckles. "That's the thing about us, Ford. When we find people we care about, we hurt them." Mercy's eyes are on Lexie, who reclines on the loveseat with her face in her iPad. "I think it's about time we made some changes before it's too late."

"I doubt she'd have me back after what I did. But I shouldn't have been so hard on you."

"You were just telling me the truth and like you I didn't want to hear it. But I'll do better. The question is...what are you going to do?"

DAMN IF IT WASN'T HOT AS HELL ON THE LAKE. IT nearly made me smile to realize I'd gone from one scorching hot climate to another. But this time, I have someone to come home to, someone who looked forward to seeing me at the end of the day.

Somehow it made all the difference. Or it would have, if I hadn't thrown it all away.

A fine day for fishing despite the heat, I had to admit. A damn fine day.

The only sounds were the slap of water against the sides of the boat, the *swish* and *plop* of the fishing line and lure with each toss and the occasional hum from the trolling motor as we skimmed the prime spots of Bear Lake.

Paul Hadley, who looks as relaxed as a man can be fixes his line with a new worm and gives it a good toss, then settles back with a fresh beer. "Man, I needed this today. Thanks for inviting me out."

"Can't say I didn't have ulterior motives, Paul."

He takes a deep drink from his beer. "They didn't make

me Sheriff for nothing. I figured you were wondering about Lola, considering I heard you and Miz Peyton are getting serious."

"I know you can't talk about an ongoing investigation," I say.

His aviators wink under the glare of the sun as he focuses his gaze in my direction. "I can't, but hypothetically, if we *were* to talk about the investigation, you'd be interested to learn the DNA from under Lola's fingernails wasn't male. It was female. Strictly off the record of course."

"No one to hear you but me and the fishes," I tell him. "Female?" I repeat after a minute of contemplation. Peyton had been so sure it was a man. It must have been a tall woman. Or someone in really tall boots.

"I'm about ready to put this mess to rest, let me tell you." He sighs, adjusts his sunglasses, and twitches his fishing rod while he waits for a bite.

I make a sound of agreement as I reel in my line. My thoughts are rolling as slow as molasses, until it hits. "Jesus H. Christ," I shout.

"Well, what the hell is that about?" Paul says indignantly. "You 'bout scared all the fish from here to Tennessee."

"Reel your line in. What do you want to bet when you run that DNA again it'll match Lola's?" I start gathering up our gear and stowing it haphazardly. "Fuck, hurry up, Beau. I have to get to Peyton."

My hands turn clammy and despite the sweltering heat, I break out in a cold sweat. For a moment, as my nose fills with the stomach churning scents of sunbaked North Carolina mud and the damp odor of rotting vegetation, I'm overcome with the same helplessness I felt in Afghanistan. The same dread of being responsible for another life and knowing there's a possibility I may feel again--with Peyton.

"Ford, man, calm down and tell me what's going on."

My gear stowed, I start helping him with his. "Who in this town would have a motive to kill Lola and is female? Who is close enough to Peyton to fuck around with her shit, make her think she's going crazy?"

Paul packs up his fishing rod and dumps the rest of his beer overboard, then throws the can in the trash. While he does that, I flip up the trolling motor and wait impatiently at the steering wheel. As soon as the rest of his gear is safely put away, I shift into gear and speed away from our peaceful little fishing spot, shattering the calm, still water with a guttural groan from the engine and a loud crash of water.

"You can't mean Alice," Paul says over the sound of the boat cutting through the waves.

"That's exactly who I mean. Christ, Paul, she's been systematically discounting Peyton's credibility so even if she did point the finger toward Alice, no one would believe her."

It takes me less than half the time to pull up to the landing than it did to get out to our spot. With the ease of many years' worth of practice, I line the boat up to the dock and slide it in.

"You wait here, I'll get the truck and the trailer."

"Goddammit, Ford. What do you think we're gonna do? Arrest Alice on suspicion?" Paul yells behind me as I leap over the side of the boat and into the murky lake water.

"I don't give a fuck what you do, Paul, but I'm going to find Peyton."

Tires spit gravel in protest when I back out of the parking spot with reckless abandon. My heart beats so fast in my chest, I'm afraid it may come right out of my mouth. I've been through a lot of shit, seen a lot of violent shit, but nothing scares me as much as the thought of realizing how good I had it with Peyton until it was too late.

Thanking God the Marines had trained me well to act under pressure, I back the truck up into the water and wait with growing impatience as Paul lines the boat up and drives it onto the trailer. He secures it with straps and I try calling Peyton's phone while I wait, noting she'd tried to reach me several times. Cursing myself for leaving it in the glovebox, I leave a message, but the growing sinking feeling in my stomach doesn't bode well.

The expression on Paul's face doesn't inspire confidence either. I lower the window at his tap. "You coming with me?"

"I don't mean to be a dick, but what exactly are you planning to do here?"

"Look, man, no disrespect, but I don't have time to argue with you about this. Why don't you pick up Jim and question him about where Alice was the night Lola was murdered. Push the angle of their affair. If you don't believe me after that, then I guess I'll be on my own."

"You can't run off and do something stupid. We don't need any vigilante justice. I'll go back to the station, get one of my deputies to pull Jim in. Let's do this the right way."

"Fine. You do that. I'm going to go get Peyton and make sure she's safe. She was supposed to work today." I spent all this time protecting her, keeping her safe, and I left her alone with a killer.

"Don't do anything stupid, Ford. I'll send a deputy to Splatters."

"I won't do anything stupid as long as you get your hand off my truck and check out what I said about Alice." The loaner I'd gotten while my Jeep was repaired didn't replace my baby, but it'd due.

He raps a knuckle against the door and finally takes a step back. "You watch yourself now."

I don't answer because I'm already speeding away, the

boat bouncing and creaking along behind me. Precious time ticks away, but I stop at the lodge on the way to The Art Shoppe to unhook the boat. I'll be able to move faster if I don't have to worry about navigating with its cumbersome weight behind me.

I get back in the truck and my phone rings as I start to pull away from the lodge. When I see Peyton's name on the caller I.D. I drop the damn thing twice before I can answer it.

"Peyton."

"No, lover boy."

My insides turn to ice. "Alice?"

"That's right."

I swipe a hand across my face as cold sweat drips down my forehead and into my eyes. "Where's Peyton?" I demand. "If you hurt her, I swear to God."

"Simmer down, Ford, or you won't see her again."

Drawing in air is a herculean task, but I force myself to listen to her. It won't do anyone any good for me to rage at Alice before she tells me what she's done with Peyton. "Please," I say through gritted teeth.

"We're at Windy Point, Ford. And my-oh-my is there a wonderful view," Alice answers.

"Please don't hurt her."

"I'm not. Yet."

The truck speeds along the unpaved road and spits up dust in my rearview. "You psycho bitch."

"I didn't want it to happen this way, Ford. You have to believe me. If Lola had left my husband alone none of this would have happened."

"And you tried to frame me for her murder." I curse under my breath as traffic out of town inches forward. Images of Peyton bloody and beaten flash through my mind rapid fire. My knuckles go white on the steering wheel.

It's Afghanistan all over again. I may not be shooting her full of a syringe of morphine, but I might as well. If anything happens to her, it'll be my fault. Goddammit, I should have made her leave when I had the chance, then none of this would have ever happened.

"No try about it, honey. Unfortunately, that's exactly what's going to happen."

Not if I have anything to say about it.

"The sheriff is already looking into your involvement, Alice. There is no way you'll get out of this." I know trying to reason with her is a waste of time, but I have to try. For Peyton.

"Who do you think they'll believe? Me, an upstanding member of the community and the former mayor's daughter or the man the whole country already knows is a murderer?"

"She was your sister."

The harsh bark of her laughter fills the speaker. "No real sister would sleep with my husband." Her otherwise calm voice sharpens. "I did everything for her. Raised her. Gave her a home after she left that shit-for-brains boyfriend of hers. Convinced Dad to make her a beneficiary in his will. She dug her own grave when she took what was mine. Just like you and Ms. Rhodes here did when you wouldn't leave well enough alone."

I flinch. "I'm almost there."

"You park your truck and come to the Point. It's closed today for maintenance so we won't be interrupted. You come unarmed now, Ford. We wouldn't want this to get ugly. No one wants that, do we?"

"No."

"We'll be waiting."

Click.

The parking lot is nearly empty when I pull in and claim a spot nearest to the trail for the Point. Much as it pains me, I leave my 9mm and backup in the glovebox and pocket my phone. Wind whistles through the trees and howls in the canyon beyond. If it were under any other circumstances, it'd be a good day for a hike, but dread clouds over the beauty.

My ears ring at the effort to listen over the noise as I trek the roped off trail the short distance to the Point. The trail tops a small crest, then veers sharply right. To my front, the steep slope of the mountain affords gorgeous views. To my left and right the trail extends in either direction with a waist-high safety barrier marking the way.

With two senses down, I'm at a distinct disadvantage and only have one option.

I don't think twice about rounding the corner for whatever my fate may be.

I COME TO, my head screaming, and crack open an eye to get my bearings. A steep drop fills my vision and I gasp, my hands attempt to reach out for an anchor, my stomach pitching. The parfait I'd had for breakfast threatens to resurface and I whimper.

"Oh, calm down. You aren't going anywhere."

Feet scuffle against concrete and I arch my neck to the side to find Alice leaning against the security fencing. "Where are we?" I ask when my brain pulses in protest.

"The Point, waiting for lover boy."

"Ford? Why? Alice you don't have to do this." My mental gears are rusty and thoughts slow. I try to move my arms and realize they're braced behind my back with a restraint.

"Don't try moving. You aren't going to get free."

"How did you get me out here? What are you planning to do?"

Alice braces herself against the bannister and studies the view beyond. "You started waking up when we got close. You did most of the work, it was just a matter of keeping you upright. All you need to know is I never intended to hurt you—either of you really. If you'd kept your nose in your own business, none of this would have had to happen."

"You don't need to involve Ford. Just take me," I plead.

"Not a chance," comes his voice and my stomach sinks. "I'm here now. I'll do what you want, Alice, but you've got to let Peyton go. She won't say a word about what happened and you can take your pound of flesh from me."

The way I'm bound, I can't turn to see him and everything inside me aches to see his face just one more time.

"Isn't that sweet?" Alice croons. "Nice and easy, now Ford. No heroics." She steps closer to my side and the cold press of a gun barrel kisses the skin at my temple.

"You don't have to have a gun to her head. I'm here. I'll do what you want."

She jams it into my skin and I cry out in pain, head still tender from the earlier blow. At my sound of pain, she slams the butt of the gun against my temple and I go limp, nearly blacking out again. I only manage to hold onto consciousness by clinging to the sound of Ford's harsh shouts of protest.

I hang limply from the post or whatever she has me tied to, my arms at an awkward angle and my shoulders throbbing in pain, but it's nothing compared to the maelstrom of hurt knocking around inside my skull. My thigh muscles quiver with the effort to hold my weight and I heave myself up to lean against the post. As Alice and Ford argue, I struggle to keep from passing out. It's only my hands knocking against a lump in my back pocket that shocks me back to clarity.

My knife.

A spurt of adrenaline kicks my thoughts back into gear and I hope Alice can't see what I'm doing as I adjust my position to fit my numb hands into my pocket. It takes a long time, longer than I thought, to fit my awkward fingers around the pocket knife. I've never been more grateful for my habit of keeping a weapon on me at all times than I am as I pull it from my jeans. It takes precious moments longer to flip open the blade.

"What do you want from us?" I hear Ford ask. His voice is closer than it had been and I realize he's standing close behind me, shielding me. My already weak knees turn to jelly.

I strain to hear above the pounding in my head and the roar of the wind to hear Alice's reply. "You two are gonna take a tumble over the Point here. They'll find your bodies... eventually. I didn't want it to come to this, but you left me no choice."

"You always have a choice. You chose to kill Lola."

"That bitch told me she was pregnant!" Alice's scream echoes inside my head and against the rock walls surrounding us.

"Lola was pregnant?" Ford asks.

"Five years I've been trying to have a baby. Five. Then she takes me out to the lake house and tells me like I should be happy for her. She was pregnant with my husband's baby and she expected me to let the two of them get away so they could live happily ever after."

"So you two went for a late night ride and you drowned her."

There's a pause and I swear the sound of the knife sawing through the rope binding my wrists together is as loud as the beat of my heart.

"I wanted to talk to her, reason with her. But there's no reasoning with Lola. There never has been. She told me she was going to have the baby no matter what I wanted. Jim deserved to be happy and they were happy together. He was going to leave me, you see, to be with her. The happy little family. I had to do it."

"She was going to make you look like a fool," Ford says.

"In front of everyone! It would have killed Mama to have such a scandal flaunted around town."

"You did what you had to do to protect her."

"Yes!" Alice says, sounding pleased to hear Ford catching on. "I couldn't let them hurt Mama, or Daddy's memory. Jim's been so upset since it happened I didn't have to kill him, too."

She's so nonchalant discussing cold-blooded murder it makes my skin crawl.

"I wish we would have known the circumstances," Ford says softly. "I would have convinced Peyton to drop the whole thing. You never meant to hurt her. You couldn't help yourself."

"I wish you would have. But you didn't. If you had, I wouldn't have had to do this. I just wanted it all to go away. For everything to go back to normal. If you two had left well enough alone it would have gone away and it would all be fine. But you didn't."

Ford makes a comforting sound in his throat. "I understand now. *We* understand. If you let us go, we'll drop it. No one will ever have to know what really happened. It can stay between us. We'll leave and your life can go back to what it was."

"Nice try, Ford, but you know I can't do that. I can't leave any loose ends. Jim and I will start over once the shock of your deaths has passed. He'll feel too guilty for cheating to leave me now. We'll use Lola's share from Daddy's death to do a round of IVF or adopt a baby and we'll be happy. As for you two, well no one will miss a killer and a runaway. It's for the best, really. Now, why don't you climb over that fence there and join Peyton. It'll be easier if you don't fight it."

"Don't go through with this, Alice. You'll regret it."

"After it's over, we'll move on and forget. It'll be like it never happened." Ford grunts and I hear the scrabble of shoes against rock as they both come closer.

My bloodless fingers drop the pocket knife and I nearly cry out in desperation. The rope is taut, but I have to hope I was able to cut through enough. I have to. I'll only get one chance and I hope I don't screw it up.

CHAPTER TWENTY SIX
FORD

THE LAST TIME I had someone's fate in my hands, I failed them. I won't fail Peyton now. I can't. Life has meaning again with her in it and I'll be damned if I lose her before I tell her that myself.

I manage to inch closer throughout our conversation. Without taking my eyes off Alice, I assess Peyton's condition through my peripheral. My chest eases when she doesn't seem to be hurt. A little worse for the wear, but she's alive.

For now.

Knowing Alice wants to keep me in her sights, I inch around until Peyton is behind me, at least a little shielded from Alice's view and away from the gun she'd had pointed at her head. If we make it out of this, I don't think I'll ever be able to erase that image from my memory.

But I'll spend every day trying.

"After it's over, we'll move on and forget. It'll be like it never happened." Alice says, then lunges forward, her eyes wild with madness, spittle flying from her open mouth. The gun is pointed in my direction, it's barrel centered in my vision.

Time slows.

My thoughts quiet.

Before I can make a move, Peyton explodes into action, stunning both me and Alice, whose hold on the gun wavers. Peyton vaults over the fence, stumbling and losing her balance as her full weight lands on her bloodless legs. She tumbles into a heap with a moan. While Alice is distracted, I lock onto her waist and shove her against the opposite barrier.

"Go!" I shout to Peyton over Alice's screams of protest. "Get the fuck out of here."

Peyton gets to her knees, her lip bloody and bruised and her body covered in dust and grit. "What about you?" she asks.

"Go!" I repeat instead of answering because I know it wouldn't have been an answer she would have liked.

As Peyton takes her first steps, Alice lunges in my grasp, but Peyton is already bolting around the rock face, her footsteps pounding in the distance until they're too faint to hear.

"You son of a bitch," Alice growls. I pin her back against the rock wall although only half of my attention is on her. The rest is straining to hear if Peyton is far enough away to be safe. Which is a critical error.

Only I realize it too late.

Alice drops down to her knees abruptly, causing me to lose my balance. We scrabble for control of the gun that skitters across the bumpy concrete. She reaches it first.

I see the decision in her eyes before she pulls the trigger. It's been years since I've been shot, but goddamn it feels exactly like I remember. The bullet tears into my shoulder and I go down, spinning and crashing into the rock. The last thing I hear as I fade in and out of consciousness is the sound of Alice following Peyton.

I hear Cal shouting my name as clearly as I did the last night I saw him, when everything went to shit. The pain floods over me until I'm not sure where I am or even *when* I am. The gritty, earthy taste of dirt fills my mouth, my nose, seems to coat my lungs the way it used to when I was in the desert. It's the memory of losing a brother, a life I'd been tasked to protect, that pulls me back to the present.

When I can find my voice, the first word that comes to mind is her name. I don't know if I speak it or shout it, but it claws out of my throat leaving it as raw as the wound in my shoulder.

I sit up too quickly, my head throbs in protest. It feels

like it's going to collapse on itself, but pure instinct has me fighting against waves of nausea. With what remaining strength I have, I pull myself up. My right hand is near useless from the shoulder wound. I get to my feet by leveraging my weight onto my left side and hanging onto the fence post for dear life. My nerveless legs wobble like a fucking newborn deer, but I manage to stay upright.

My whole body aches and I'd rather be run over by a MAC truck than take another step, but I have to. All I can think of is Peyton's face, bone white with fear, as she turned to flee.

With Alice, gun drawn and following close behind.

The inspiration of nightmares. My nightmares.

The very thing I'd fought so hard to keep from happening again has happened.

I pull off my t-shirt one-handed, leaving me in a thin wife-beater soaked in my own blood, and rip a strip from the arm. I lose a lot of time wrapping the cloth around the still-seeping wound, but I know if I don't at least staunch the flow of blood, I'll be useless. When it's as bandaged as it's going to be, I grit my teeth.

I inch my way up the path, supporting my weight against the handrail, thankful the shot had been a through and through, at least. Alice had been so blood-hungry, she hadn't stopped to check and see if I was down for good. At least that's one thing in my favor.

If Cal were really here he'd tell me to man the fuck up. It's just a scratch.

Because his voice still rings all too clearly in my ear, I white-knuckle it up the path, ignoring the pulsing burn emanating from my shoulder. My ears strain for signs of life, for anything. But it's as quiet as a funeral. The kind of quiet that makes all my not-so-forgotten instincts light up like crazy.

My truck sits in the parking lot where I left it. Alice's SUV—I hadn't paid much attention when I pulled in—is parked next to it.

"Peyton!" Alice calls from somewhere in the forest beyond the parking lot. "You're gonna break your pretty neck running around like this. Come back so we can talk about it."

I dive into the brush, crashing through the scrub and trees like a belligerent bear. I don't give a fuck. Let her come. Better me than her.

Better me than her.

Stumbling over a root, I go crashing to the ground, my wound screaming, and I nearly black out. When I get to my knees, it's with a gun to my head.

"Well, if I can't get her on my own, at least I can use you to find her. People will do anything for love." She jams the gun against my back. "Get up."

I do as she says, but I inch toward the treeline hoping

Peyton is running deeper into the forest, away from Alice. I'd die happily if it meant she could live.

"You've got me, just let her go."

Alice digs the gun into my ribs. "Not a chance."

My heart clenches in my chest. "Please, Alice. I'll do whatever you want."

"What is it about these women that gets you men so wrapped around their fingers? Is it the sex? The *drama*?"

I lift a shoulder then instantly regret it. "You want me to explain it to you?"

"We've got all the time in the world. Tell me, Ford, I want to know. How is it she got you so under her spell? She reminds me so much of my sister. At first I thought it was a cosmic joke. They're both pretty, petite, blonde. Tell me is it her looks?"

"It's everything, Alice, though I doubt you'd understand. She's my person. So if you're planning on pulling that trigger you better pull it now before I send you to hell for what you've put her through."

"Such a hero," Alice snarls.

An engine revs, sounding like a plane coming to land it's so loud. I throw myself down to the ground more out of muscle memory than intention. A streak passes in front of my vision and at first I think I'm going to pass out—which would have really pissed me off—but it's Peyton in my truck, gunning the engine and aiming straight for Alice.

In the split second before the truck crashes into her, Alice raises her gun, madness bright in her eyes, and fires three times in rapid succession.

I move too quickly then, knocking my shoulder against a tree in my haste and someone flicks off the lights.

"FORD? FORD, HONEY, IT'S PEYTON. CAN YOU HEAR me?" I scowl at her nagging. This woman will be the death of me. "That's it. Come back to me."

I know I should open my eyes, but I'm terrified to find that her voice is a dream. When I do manage to sack up and look up. I find Peyton leaning over me, her face wracked with worry. "Hey there, sunshine."

Laughter bubbles up and she sobs, falling over my chest. "I'm so glad you're here."

"Me, too. For a second there, I thought I wouldn't be." I manage to sit up. "Where's Alice?"

Peytons eyes cloud over. "The ambulance took her. Hadley showed up about five minutes after...after. They weren't sure if she was going to make it. Her husband was with him. He tried to climb in the ambulance and hurt her for killing Lola."

I'd laugh, but it'd hurt to much. "I think I've had enough excitement for one day. Go easy on me," I say as I gather her into my arms. "I won't ever be able to get that image out of my head..." I'm horrified to find my voice cracking.

"Sure you will," she says. Her words are so soft, I have to lean closer to hear. "That is, if you'll have me. I'd like to spend the rest of my life making new memories to replace these."

I shake my head and she frowns. "Why not?" she asks.

"I wouldn't change the past few months with you for anything," I tell her. "Though I wouldn't have waited so long to get you back in bed."

She laughs, then winces. "*That's* what you're thinking about?"

"No, what I'm thinking about is that I almost lost you when I'd just found you. That I came so close to never getting to tell you how I feel about you."

"Ford," she whispers.

I pull her down and taste the salt on her lips. "I love you, Peyton," I say and I've never been so sure about anything in my life. She's the rock that's kept me from drifting away. The certainty in a life full of unknowns. The calm in the middle of desert sandstorm and I don't want to live another day without her knowing it.

THREE MONTHS LATER

"I KNEW IT," Peyton says, her voice ringing out over the shouts of children and the sounds of splashing water. "You're trying to kill me. This whole time I thought you were trying to help me, but nooo."

I glance down at her and hold back a laugh. Her blonde hair is matted against her head and draped over her shoulders like tentacles. Her blood-shot eyes shoot daggers as I say, "If I wanted to kill you, I could have saved myself the trouble and let you drown the first time."

Her fingers dig into my biceps even though I've got her securely by the waist. "I think it's your long game. You lulled me into a false sense of security and now that I'm not expecting it, you're going to go for the throat."

Pulling her closer to me, I bring her ear to my lips. "I could think of other ways I could torture you that would be much more pleasurable."

Peyton slaps my arm, but I don't miss the way her breath shudders out of her. "Stop playing. I'm trying to concentrate."

"It's not rocket science, sunshine."

"So says you."

"So says the five-year-old behind you who is literally swimming laps around you."

Her head whips around and she flushes prettily. "Clearly that child is a prodigy. Notify the U.S. Olympic team. We've found the next Phelps."

"Stop worrying about it. I've got you. I won't let anything happen to you."

She eyes the water with blatant mistrust. "It's not you I'm worrying about. It's what lurks beneath the murky depths that scares me."

"Nothing down there but fish and frogs wondering what the hell you're doing on dry land."

"If you must know, I'm currently deciding whether or not I should risk dunking your head under water. The thought terrifies me, but it would give me immense satisfaction."

I step in front of her, blocking her view of the lake and guide her gaze up to mine. "You have nothing to worry about. I'll be here the whole time. All you have to do is hold onto me."

Her body softens and her grip eases on my arms. "Okay, okay, fine." She grimaces, then takes a step forward. Guided by my hold, I ease her a couple feet into the water, going slowly so she can acclimate.

"Thank you for not throwing me in," she says as we pause.

My grin is slow in response. "I don't mind at all, baby. I've got the best view in the place. You in that swimsuit is all the motivation I need and you can take all the time you want."

"You're terrible."

"And you're stuck with me."

As we wade deeper into the water her breathing grows shallow. "That fact has never been more evident considering you've got my life in your hands."

"It wouldn't be the first time." But it is the first where the thought doesn't send me running scared. Instead, I want to hold her closer. I want to let her know she can always count on me to be there for her, that she can trust me to stick when shit gets slippery. "So tell me," I say to distract her, "how is it you never learned how to swim?"

She squints into the sunlight, diamonds of water dripping off all her delectable curves. "I was one of those girly girls who stuck to the beach and worked on my tan."

"Damn shame," I say.

"Why's that?"

"Cause you sure as hell look good all wet."

"Don't get me all worked up."

I chuckle. "We'll save that for after you swim."

"You're very optimistic today. What's with that? Where's my pessimistic grouch?"

"He's on vacation. I've got a pretty girl, a cold beer waiting in a cooler, and some fish with my name on them. I'm thinking fish fry tomorrow. Maybe we invite Mercy and Lexie over, Nell and her family. Make it a whole thing."

"We should invite Hadley, too. He deserves it after we gave him such a hard time the past couple months."

"Well, alright then." When I tug on her arms she comes with me, her weight resting on my chest as I take us deeper into the water. "That's it, baby. I've got you. Just let your legs float up. I'm not gonna let anything happen to you."

Her arms wrap around my shoulders and I have to admit I could get used to these swimming lessons. I'll take any excuse to have her half-naked body pressed against mine.

"I have something to talk to you about. I figure now is a good time since I've got a good hold on you so you won't be able to run away."

"I'm not going anywhere, so why don't we give floating a try."

She squints at me again. "You're not allowed to make a quick escape, Ford Collier."

"I won't." I help her flip over and steady her with my hands splayed over her spine. "The trick is to relax your body, it does most of the work for you. If you start to sink, arch your spine a little and bend your knees. That's it. You're doing great."

"I like having you as my own personal cheerleader. I could get used to it. Did they teach that in the Marines?"

"Keep talking," I tell her and then whisper all the filthy things I can do to that smart mouth if she keeps it up.

When I finish, her skin is flushed, but it isn't from the sun. She clears her throat. "*Anyway*, I got a phone call from Uncle Brad today. The lawyer who embezzled the rest of the funds from my parent's accounts has been charged and the emergency relief fund generated by the bar associations for these sort of circumstances is cutting me a check for the amount he stole."

My eyes trail down her tight stomach and the flare of her hips. "That's great news. I'm happy for you."

"Would you still be happy if I told you I was going to stay in Windy Point? Permanently."

The breath rushes out of me and I study her serene expression intently. "Permanently?"

Her hands make lazy angel wings on the surface of the water. "That's right. After Alice was convicted, you know her husband put the business up for sale. It seems he's going to move back to his hometown up north."

My throat goes tight. "I heard that somewhere. Small towns, you know."

A smile plays at her lips. "I've heard that somewhere. Anyway, I decided to buy it using the money from the trust. I'm going to reopen it doing the same things, but also offer children's classes, art showings from local artists. I have a ton of ideas."

"You're staying?" I manage, all jokes aside. I hadn't given much thought to what would happen after everything settled down. In the moment, I'd only been concerned about keeping Peyton alive, and then about enjoying what time I had with her. I couldn't ask her to put her life on hold for me, not when she was finally enjoying her freedom again. The last thing I wanted to do was put her in a cage.

"Of course I'm staying. My life is here."

"The business is a great opportunity for you. I'm proud of you."

She gets to her feet, faces me. "I wasn't talking about the business, although that's one part of it. I was talking about you."

Suddenly, I'm the one afraid, although it's not because of the water. "Me?"

"That is, if you'll have me?" Her eyes shine up at me

and I wonder what I did to deserve someone so perfect for me in every way.

I cup her jaw and brush my lips over hers. "I was going to ask you at some point, but I wanted to give you time. I guess you beat me to it."

"You were taking too long and I got impatient when I saw the way you were looking at me. You aren't mad that I didn't let you be the dashing hero and let you ask me first?"

"I don't give a damn about that. All I want is you, any and every way I can have you."

"I love you, Ford. So much," she says against my mouth. "I don't want to go a day without saying that to you."

"And I don't want to go a day without you."

Tears slide down her cheeks and she brushes them away with her fingers. "I'm not going to cry and since today is a day for firsts—the first day of the rest of our lives together, because now you're stuck with me—I'm going to swim."

I squeeze her hand to let her know I'll be here, whenever she needs me. With a deep inhalation, she dives into the waist-deep water and begins to kick her feet. Her first attempts are more error than success, but with each trial, she goes a little deeper, stays up a little longer.

By the time the sun starts its descent and most of the other people have cleared out, she's streaking through the water like a dolphin and I've retreated to the chairs set halfway in the gentle waves for my first beer. I'd planned on fishing hours ago, but that can wait for tomorrow. There's plenty of time for solitude, I've had enough of that for one lifetime anyway.

Speaking of solitude, I think of the contents of the box Tate's family had forwarded to me. I'd called his mother when I finally got the balls to open it and we spent some time remembering Ryan. She asked me what it was like when he died and I told her the truth. He'd fallen asleep and it was as peaceful as any one of us could have wished. When she thanked me, she asked that I pass along the contents of the box to the appropriate parties. Considering it was the least I could do, the package and its contents were now on their way to Cal, who'd either kill me or worse when he realized who it was from.

But I'd deal with it either way, because I wasn't alone anymore and I never would be again.

When Peyton comes back to me to sit in my lap and kiss me crazy, then bounds off to dive back into the water, I realize she needed someone to give her room to breathe and I needed someone who'd stick no matter how much I tried to push them away.

As her laughter rings in my ears, I relax back into my chair. If every day from now until my dying day is a repeat of this one, I'd go to the grave a happy man.

SWEET CREEK, TENNESSEE

CAL, the package begins, *I know you don't much want to hear from me, but I figure someone has to man up and be the one to reach out and it may as well be me. I know how you feel about me and I understand, but there are some things you should know.*

If my gut is right, and you may disagree, but you may not, then you may be in danger. I would have called or emailed, but I wasn't sure if you'd have taken it. Everything you need to know is in this package. If you want me to drop it, I will, but Ryan deserved better. We all did.

I'm available if you want to talk.

Miss you, brother. Be well.

Ford

Twin flames of grief ignite in my chest as the piece of paper with the familiar scribble crumples in my hand. The box lay innocently on my stoop, an unwelcome reminder of a past I want nothing more than to forget.

I down the beer I'm drinking and unlock the door, then kick the package through with the toe of my boot. It skids across the scuffed wood floor and lands underneath the jutting expanse of the bar. I leave it there like a live grenade that I want fuck all to do with.

Instead, I get another beer after tossing the other and retreat to my favorite recliner and turn on a random sports channel for the white noise. I drink two more before my phone rings, interrupting the buzz I'm trying to work on.

When I see the name on the phone, I consider ignoring it, too. Must be a day for blasts from the past, but I have no real interest in a history lesson.

When the number calls again, I sigh and answer.

"Hello, Gwen," I say and even saying her name has me going for beer number four.

When she speaks, I trade the beer for whiskey.

Hard liquor is the only way to deal with ghosts and the woman who ground your heart under her worn red cowboy boots like it was nothing.

Operator

Last to Leave, Book Two

This elite group of U.S. Marines are the last to leave a fight...or the women who steal their hearts.

He's the one man she never wanted to see again.

It's been five years since Gwen Winston laid eyes on the man who took her virginity—and broke her heart. Five years since he told her he could never see her again—right after she married his brother. Now he's back, a year after her husband's death to pay his respects. The cause of death was suicide—but he doesn't believe it.

Once Gwen's life is threatened, she begins to doubt everything she thought was true...including how wrong it would be to get close to Callum Reece.

She's the one woman he can't have.

Callum "Cal" Reece is at loose ends after losing the only family he had left and leaving the Marines. When he sees Gwen again for the first time in years, all he can think about is how much he missed her while he'd been deployed on back-to-back missions, even if she's his brother's widow. Wanting her is wrong. Needing her is worse...but losing her is unthinkable.

Sometimes the forbidden is a dangerous temptation.

When they give into a passion they can't deny and uncover secrets determined to tear them apart, Gwen and Cal realize it will take learning to forgive to survive.

I'm so excited to finally introduce you to a new bunch of kickass men. The *Last to Leave* series has been percolating in my brain for a while now and I can't wait for you to meet all the new guys.

If you enjoyed reading, please consider leaving a review at your preferred retailer.

Keep your eyes peeled for the next book in the series!

Thank you for all of your support,

Nicole

ACKNOWLEDGMENTS

This book wouldn't be here without the help of some very important people in my life.

To my mother. For holding my hand this past year even though I wanted to do everything myself. Thank you for helping me when I needed it the most. I may be a pain in the ass, but I love you to the moon and back and always will.

To my brothers. The past ten years, we've all be doing our own thing and for the first time in a long time, it's nice to be on the same track, in the same area. I love the men you've become and I'm so very grateful to have you both in my life. You've both shown me there will always be someone in my corner. And that you're always available for a strong back or a kind word. You're the best!

To my daughter. I do everything with you and mind and sometimes, I have to just cross my fingers and hope the choices I've made are the right ones. I hope one day you'll look back and say I've been a good mom. Each day I want to quit, you remind me how important it is to keep going. In a world full of darkness, you are the light.

To Alana. I mean, I think you in every book, but it honestly will never be enough for all that you've done for me in the **five** years we've known each other. I continue to be grateful for your helping hand and your sympathetic ear.

To Melissa. Who is always there if I need to bounce an idea or need someone to cheer me on. I don't even know what you get out of listening to me go on and on about these books, but I'm thankful that you take the time out of your busy day to listen and to give your thoughtful opinions. A lot of words wouldn't be written without your endless encouragement.

To my friends from Nicole's Knockouts who have stood by me every step of the way, thank you for your support and patience. I know I say it all the time, but you are the reason why I put fingers to keys and make these books a reality. You always seem to know just when I want to throw in the towel and are there with an encouraging word and a listening ear. Sometimes I think I'm alone in this journey and then I look up and all of you are there to remind me I'm not.

To each and every blogger who helps spread the word.

Thank you for your tireless dedication and unwavering support!

Thank you to Letitia Hasser from R.B.A Designs for helping me format the paperback cover. You're an angel!

Thank you to Jenn Wood from All About the Edits for taking a girl on last minute and rocking the hell out of this book.

To Jessica Neilson, Cindy Camp, Teri Hicks, Vera Green, Rhonda Brant, and Kristin Youngblood. I can't thank you enough for beta reading Traitor when it was raw and new and helping me to make it shine.

Last but not least, thank you to each and every one of you for reading!

 **Nicole Blanchard** is the *New York Times* and *USA Today* bestselling author of gritty romantic suspense and heartwarming new adult romance. She and her family reside in the south along with their two spunky Boston Terriers and one chatty cat. Visit her website www.authornicoleblanchard.com for more information or to subscribe to her newsletter for updates on sales and new releases.

facebook.com/authornicoleblanchard

twitter.com/blanchardbooks

instagram.com/authornicoleblanchard

amazon.com/Nicole-Blanchard

bookbub.com/authors/nicole-blanchard

goodreads.com/nicole_blanchard

ALSO BY NICOLE BLANCHARD

First to Fight Series

Anchor

Warrior

Survivor

Savior

Honor

Box Set: Books 1-5

Last to Leave Series

Traitor

Operator

Aviator

Captor

Protector

Immortals Ever After Series

Deal with a Dragon

Vow to a Vampire

Fated to a Fae King

Dark Romance

Toxic

Fatal

Friend Zone Series

Friend Zone

Frenemies

Friends with Benefits

Standalone Novellas

Bear with Me

Darkest Desires

Mechanical Hearts

CPSIA information can be obtained
at www.ICGtesting.com
Printed in the USA
BVHW03s1309251018
531100BV00033B/639/P

9 781635 762297